C000121588

Mocha
and Murder

Holly Holmes Cozy Culinary Mystery –
book 6

K.E. O'Connor

K.E. O'Connor Books

MOCHA CREAM AND MURDER

Copyright © 2021 K.E. O'Connor.

ISBN: 978-1-9163573-5-8

Written by K.E. O'Connor

Edited by Amy Hart

Cover design by Stunning Book Covers

Beta read by my wonderful early review team. You're all amazing.

Chapter 1

"You should come with me to take a look." Granny Molly pushed her plate away and patted her stomach. "I'd like your opinion on the place."

"You don't have to move out of here if you don't want to. There's no hurry." I stood to take our empty plates from the table, but Gran waved at me to stay sitting.

"I'll wash up. After all, you cooked such a delicious meal. I've never tasted such incredible roast potatoes."

"You mean, I did an amazing job of reheating leftovers I snuck out of the kitchen because it was only going to be thrown away." That was one of the many benefits of working at Audley Castle. You were always guaranteed delicious food.

Gran grabbed the empty plates and carried them to the sink, her newly acquired dog, Saffron, glued to her heel. "Holly, I want to do my bit while I'm living under your roof."

"I really don't mind you staying longer." I'd enjoyed having Gran back. She'd been out of my life for too long.

"As sweet as your apartment is, you only have one bedroom. And I can't keep getting under your feet. Plus, Meatball is having to put up with this little madam's sass."

She looked down at Saffron. "Besides, it's not as if you invited me to stay." She turned and smiled, her warm, open face taking me back to the fun we had together when I was growing up.

"I feel like I've only just got you back, and you're leaving already."

"We'll have none of that nonsense. And I didn't exactly have a choice but to leave you. I had the offer of a comfortable single bed in a delightful prison cell. I could hardly turn that down."

I shook my head. As much as I loved Gran, I didn't love her inability to avoid getting involved in dodgy deals. It was something she was working on.

"I'm happy to come look at the place with you. It's on the corner of the village green, isn't it?" I said.

"Yes. I'll have a great view of all the comings and goings of the locals. I could even make some new friends."

"You already have a new friend. Ray. I thought maybe you'd take him along to have a look, since you're getting along well."

A faint blush rose on her cheeks. Gran was an attractive older lady with a good figure. It was no surprise she still had guys chasing after her.

She turned away and ran water into the sink. "We are getting along well, but we don't need to rush things."

"Maybe you should. You're not getting any younger."

She flicked soap suds at me. "Less of your cheek. There's plenty of life left in these bones."

A knock at the front door of my apartment had us turning.

Gran checked the time on the wall clock. "It's getting late. Are you expecting a visitor?"

I shook my head as I walked to the door. Meatball, my adorable corgi-cross, was right by my heels. Saffron was close behind, always keen to see what was going on.

"No. Let's see who it is." I pulled open the door.

Chef Heston stood there looking flushed. "There's a kitchen emergency. You're needed."

"Good evening to you, too." Gran wandered over, drying her hands on a towel.

He flicked a gaze her way. "Good evening. Well, Holly. Let's get a move on."

"What's the emergency?" I was already reaching for my jacket.

"Not so fast, young man." Gran stood with her hands on her hips, while Saffron growled at Chef Heston. "My granddaughter has been working hard for you all day. What gives you the right to turn up unannounced and demand she does overtime?"

"Um, well, he is my boss," I said, not keen on making Chef Heston angry. It never ended well for me.

"He could be Tutankhamen. Manners cost nothing," Gran said. "Not so much as a please or thank you, just barking orders. No wonder he's not married."

"Gran!"

She nodded. "No woman would put up with that bad behavior for long."

He grumbled under his breath. "You can have tomorrow morning off if you must. But I expect you to be back in the afternoon."

"Really?" It was rare to get an offer like that. The hours in the kitchen at Audley Castle were long and people were expected to be flexible.

"Only if you come right away," he said.

"What do you need her for?" Gran stood her ground.

"There's been a … mix up with an order for the party at Marchwood Manor. I just had word that they're short on the desserts."

"We've got plenty of options in the chiller cabinets. I can zoom some over in the van," I said.

3

"If it were that easy, I'd have done it myself," Chef Heston said. "Sir Richard Marchwood insisted on your special chocolate mocha cream cake. He said he'd been dreaming about it for days and was so disappointed when it didn't show up in the order."

"He should have thought about that when he put in the order," Gran said.

"He did," I said. "I remember seeing the order. He wanted thirty mini chocolate mocha cream cakes. I even wrote it on the task order for the day. Oh! Then … someone rubbed it all out."

"Really! Who would that someone be?" Gran glared at Chef Heston.

He shuffled his feet. "It's not important. We can't let our customers down."

"I think it's crucially important. Was it you by any chance, Chef Heston?" Gran said.

He grumbled several times but confessed to nothing.

I glanced at him and bit my lip. I didn't have the neatest handwriting, and Chef Heston was a stickler for everything being in order. I'd been in a hurry when I'd dashed down the tasks for the day on the board we used to check our work duties. I remembered writing down the chocolate mocha cream cake order. It was one of my favorites, and I'd planned to make an extra batch to share with Princess Alice.

Chef Heston cleared his throat. "Perhaps I did miss it off the list when I wrote out the baking tasks for the day. But Holly should have remembered."

I opened my mouth to protest, but Gran got there first. "That's not her job. You're in charge of the kitchen, and you wrote out the information incorrectly. You should make the cakes since it was your error."

"I would, but Sir Richard insists Holly does it. She's got herself something of a reputation when it comes to desserts around Audley St. Mary." Chef Heston sounded both annoyed and proud.

He should be proud. My hard work and amazing cakes reflected well on him and the castle. Not that he'd ever admit to it.

Gran smiled and threw an arm around my shoulders. "She has a magic touch when it comes to desserts. I taught her everything."

"Gran! I went to catering college."

"Well, I taught you the basics. I got you on the right track. And here you are, the queen of chocolate mocha cake in this beautiful place. You even have posh lords and ladies insisting you bake for them. They'll have you over at Buckingham Palace next, providing the desserts for the Queen."

"I'd love that. I wonder if she likes chocolate mocha cream cake," I said.

"I read somewhere she's partial to a chocolate biscuit cake," Gran said.

"I'll have to look up the recipe, just in case."

Chef Heston sighed.

I grinned. We'd let him squirm enough.

"I don't mind making the cakes," I said. "I didn't have anything planned for this evening, and we've just finished dinner."

"I suppose I can allow you to go," Gran said.

I chuckled and shook my head. "You're going on a date with Ray in half an hour. My only plans were the couch and a cuddle with Meatball. As much fun as that can be, I love any excuse to bake."

"You really need to be baking now," Chef Heston said. "The party has already started."

"The cakes won't take long to make. They'll bake quickly. I can have them over there by the time the party gets in full swing. None of the guests will miss them."

"Sir Richard missed them." Chef Heston gestured out the door.

"Because of your mistake," Gran said.

"Fine. It was my mistake. Holly, I need your chocolate mocha cream cake now."

"I'm on it." And I was always happy to help Sir Richard Marchwood. He was a kind man with a twinkle in his eye, and always generous when it came to tips. "You behave yourself on your date with Ray." I kissed Gran's cheek.

"He's always the perfect gent, no matter how much I try to convince him otherwise."

I arched an eyebrow at her. "I'm glad to hear it. He sounds like the perfect guy for you, making sure you stay on the straight and narrow."

Chef Heston tapped his foot and spent several seconds looking at his watch.

"You've made your point. Holly's coming with you," Gran said. "You can give her a minute to sort herself out."

"I'll wait outside." He slunk into the gloom.

I shrugged on my jacket, pulled on my boots, and grabbed my purse. "Meatball, do you want to stay here or come with me to your kennel?"

He was instantly up, wagging his tail. Any excuse to get outside.

"It's getting chilly out. I'll take an extra blanket so you're nice and cozy." I grabbed a few dog treats from the drawer, and an extra thick blanket that was one of his favorites, and hurried out.

Chef Heston was pacing outside, his hands twisted together. "Get a move on."

I said goodbye to Gran and then had to speed walk to catch up with him. "Do you know what the party at Marchwood Manor is for?"

"I don't question our customers why they want our desserts."

"Sir Richard is always having parties," I said. "He's really livened up the village since he bought Marchwood Manor. Didn't he move from Appledore?"

"Yes."

"That's only a few miles from here. I wonder why he moved."

"As I said, it's not my business to question customers."

"You're not the tiniest bit curious about him? His whole family seem really friendly. I don't think he's married, though."

"No, I'm not remotely curious about him. Neither should you be." Chef Heston sighed. "Not that it's your concern, but I believe it's his son having a party, not Sir Richard."

"Oh! I didn't know Jacob was home."

"You're on first name terms with Sir Richard's son?"

"Well, I don't really know him. I've met him a few times when I've made deliveries for Sir Richard. Jacob is always polite."

Chef Heston shook his head and tutted.

"What? There's nothing wrong with being nice to the customers."

"You're overly friendly. You're the same with the family."

We'd had this discussion before. Chef Heston considered me too close to the Audley family who lived in the castle. It wasn't as if I deliberately ingratiated myself with them. I'd simply clicked with Princess Alice. And as for Lord Rupert Audley, well, things were a bit more complicated there.

We walked the rest of the way in silence.

I quickly snuggled Meatball into his kennel outside the kitchen door and gave him his treats. "You be good. No barking. I won't be long, then we can go for a fun ride over to the big manor house." I dashed into the kitchen, washed up, and put on my apron.

"The oven's already heated. The ingredients are out. You just need to work your magic," Chef Heston said.

"You could help by mixing the cream." I was already measuring out flour and sugar into a large mixing bowl. I'd made my chocolate mocha cream cake so many times I could do it with my eyes closed.

Chef Heston snorted. "I'm not your commis chef. I've got work to do."

I lifted a hand. "It was just a suggestion. It could speed things up."

"I'll be in the office, sorting out the work schedule." He turned and stomped away.

Chef Heston hated being told he'd made a mistake. And he especially hated making a mistake with customers' orders. Audley Castle had an amazing reputation for creating fantastic food, and he was determined it would stay that way.

The ingredients were soon combined, and I placed the rich chocolatey mix into mini muffin tins and placed them in the oven.

I whipped the cream, cocoa powder, fresh shavings of dark chocolate, and a dash of vanilla to make the filling, then placed the bowls and mixing equipment in the industrial sized dishwasher.

The oven timer pinged. The cakes were ready. To speed things up, I left them on the side for five minutes before placing them in a chiller cabinet. If I put the cream in the cakes when they were warm, it would run right through and sit at the bottom in a sludgy lump.

While the cakes were cooling, I made thirty cream-colored miniature flowers for the decoration, and was wondering about a late night cup of tea, when Chef Heston strode back in.

"Everything ready to go?"

"Almost. I just need to put the finishing touches on the top of the cakes." I slid them into the presentation boxes and added more chocolate shavings and the tiny iced flowers.

Chef Heston peered over my shoulder. "They'll do. I've got the van out. You can drive over to the manor house."

"Are you sure? You usually make me take the bike when it's not a big order."

"We're short on time." He handed me the keys.

I was tempted to use Gran's argument and say he should make the delivery since it was his fault Sir Richard's son didn't have his cakes. But I always loved visiting Marchwood Manor. It was practically a mansion and sat on a slight hill in ten acres of pristine gardens. I also loved my job and didn't want to lose it.

"No problem. I'll zoom over there and be right back." I took off my apron and shrugged into my jacket.

"I, um, I appreciate your hard work, Holly." Chef Heston nodded at me before leaving the kitchen.

It was as close to a thank you as I was going to get, and I was happy to take it. Chef Heston had taught me a lot since I joined the kitchen at Audley Castle. Sure, he could be gruff, sometimes downright rude, and was prone to being a bit shouty, but he was a decent boss.

I opened the van, placed the cakes inside, and made sure they were secure. I whistled. "Come on, Meatball. We have a delivery to make."

He raced out of his kennel and hopped into the passenger seat of the van, while I climbed in the other side.

We were soon on our way, driving along the winding private road that led away from the castle and onto the small lanes of Audley St. Mary.

It was almost eight-thirty by the time I arrived at the manor house. It was lit up with beautiful twinkling lights around the driveway. More lights blazed from the downstairs rooms.

I parked the van close to the main door and was pulling out the boxes of cake when the door opened.

"Is that you, Holly?" Sir Richard Marchwood strolled out, wearing what must have been a custom made navy blue suit with a white shirt underneath.

"Good evening, Sir Richard. I'm here on a cake run. I heard you were missing some items from your order."

"I'm so glad you could bring them." He looked down at the glass of champagne in his hand and placed it on the window ledge. He hurried over to take the boxes.

"It's fine. I've got them."

"No, I insist. I won't stand by and see a lady fetching and carrying. Besides, I have the muscles for the job." He winked at me. "I also get a chance to nab a few cakes before my son and his greedy friends get hold of them."

I chuckled. "I don't mind doing it. It is sort of my job."

"Even so, we have to do the right thing." He took the boxes. "Sadly, I can't lay claim to all of them. Jacob's got a few of his old school friends over."

"That must be nice for him."

"I thought it would be, but the party's not going so well. There's been a couple of no-shows, and when I ducked my head in the drawing room, everyone seemed very gloomy."

"Hopefully, my cakes will cheer things up."

"As delicious as I'm sure they are, it might take more than cake to fix this social faux pas. This way." He led me into the house through the main entrance. The hallway, which was bigger than my whole apartment, was tastefully decorated with antique vases and large oil paintings of the countryside on the walls.

I followed him into an impressive granite and marble kitchen and looked around. "Would you like me to plate up the cakes?"

"Absolutely. And your timing is perfect. Most of the other nibbly bits have gone." Sir Richard tapped his fingers on the counter. "Actually, if you don't have any plans this evening, you could do more than just sort out the dessert."

I carefully placed the cakes on a plate. "Of course. What do you need? I can serve them to your guests if you want me to."

"Definitely not. I'd like you to join the party. A cheerful face is what my son needs to lighten the mood."

"Oh! I'm not sure about that. I mean …" I gestured at the cakes and then my jeans.

"Oh, Holly, you look stunning, and you'd be helping me out. I asked Jacob if there was a problem, but he said nothing was wrong. He seemed cheerful enough, but the others, well, something needs to happen, or this party will be a damp squib."

"Won't it be awkward if I simply show up?"

"Not at all. You're friendly, have a charming smile, and can woo anyone with those desserts." He winked at me again. "And I have a reputation to keep when it comes to parties. If people aren't talking about it a week after it's happened, I've done something wrong."

I bit my bottom lip. "I can't gate crash your son's party."

"He'd be thrilled to have you there. I want Jacob to enjoy himself."

The kitchen door was pushed open. Lord Rupert Audley appeared.

I was so surprised to see him, I almost dropped the tray of cakes I'd just picked up. "Hello! I didn't know you were here."

"Ah, Rupert. Come over here. I'm trying to convince the lovely Holly to join the party," Sir Richard said.

Rupert strolled over, a broad smile on his handsome face and his blue eyes sparkling. "That's the perfect idea. You must come, Holly."

"I don't really know anyone there," I said.

"You know me," Rupert said. "And have you got Meatball with you?"

"Always."

"Even better. He'll add some fun to the party. No one can resist him."

Sir Richard clapped his hands together. "Yes! Bring in your dog. Everyone will have fun petting him. We've got to do something to liven things up. What do you say, Rupert?"

"I say yes. Holly must come to the party." Rupert's grin had my resolve wavering. "Jacob won't mind you joining in. I only got an invitation at the last minute because he needed to make up the numbers."

"No! It's not just because of that. We hold your family in the highest regard," Sir Richard said. "Although the extra body definitely doesn't do any harm. I'm glad you could come."

"So am I. And the food is excellent." Rupert gestured at the tray. "Are those your chocolate mocha cream cakes I see?"

"They are," I said.

"Holly makes such incredible cakes," Rupert said.

"I know. I'm always sneaking in orders at the castle kitchen," Sir Richard said. "Holly, I insist you stay for a glass of champagne and one of your cakes. I won't hear otherwise."

Rupert caught hold of my arm and gave it a gentle squeeze. "Please stay. It would mean the world to me."

When he put it like that, I could hardly refuse. "Okay, I'll stay."

Chapter 2

"I'm not dressed for a party." I looked down at my jeans and pale blue sweater. There was a smear of flour on the hem, which I swiftly rubbed off.

"You're fine as you are. You always look pretty." Rupert walked along beside me as we headed to the van to get Meatball. "No one's dressed up."

"You are. That's one of your favorite suits." I always liked it when he wore that suit. It made his blue eyes pop.

"You like it?"

"It suits you." I laughed. "Which makes sense, since it is a suit."

He chuckled along with me. "People won't notice what you're wearing. They'll all be captivated by your cakes and conversation. Besides, there are only a few guests here. It's very low key."

"Jacob's school friends?"

"That's right. Although some of them couldn't make it."

I unlocked the van. Meatball launched out as if jet propelled. He greeted Rupert like a long-lost friend, then eyed the pristine lawn at the front of the house.

"No, you don't." I gently caught hold of his collar. "We're the entertainment for the evening. You have to be on your best behavior when we go inside. No stealing food, licking hands, or begging."

"He can do all of that. It'll only make people like him even more," Rupert said.

"Sadly, not everyone is a dog lover."

"Hmmm, I can never understand that." Rupert led the way back into the house.

"Nope. It's got me stumped, too. I'll be back in a minute." I petted Meatball, then dashed back to the kitchen, had a quick hand wash to get rid of any doggy residue, then grabbed the cakes and returned to Rupert and Meatball.

"We're in here." Rupert pushed open a dark wooden door.

I walked in ahead of him to discover a stunning room with deep jade wallpaper covered in small hummingbirds and orange flowers. A giant fireplace sat against one wall with a stylish marble mantel. Jazz music played softly in the background.

"Where shall I put the cakes?" I said.

"Over on that table should do." Rupert gestured to a long table at the side of the room.

I hurried over and set the tray down.

"They look tasty. Are they safe to eat?"

I jumped at the man's voice in my ear and turned. "Oh! Hello! I know you, don't I?"

The man had a scruffy beard, dark circles under his eyes, and messy hair. He simply stared at me and then the cakes.

Rupert hurried to my side. "Holly, this is Bruce Jonas. He used to go to school with Jacob. His school was a rival to mine."

I tilted my head as I studied Bruce. "Have we met?"

Bruce's dark eyes narrowed. "You know about me?"

"I'm trying to place you." He did look familiar.

"Rupert, I need your opinion." A guy I didn't recognize was gesturing at Rupert to join him.

"I'll be right back, Holly." Rupert nodded to me before hurrying away.

I smiled at Bruce. "Do you live in the village?"

"Possibly. Why do you want to know?" His gaze darted around the room.

"I'm just trying to remember you."

He stared at me. "You ask a lot of questions."

"Um. No, I don't. I'm being friendly. Are you enjoying the party?" Oops, there was another question.

Bruce picked up a cake and sniffed it. The cuffs of his jacket were frayed, and he had what could be mushy peas in his beard.

"Do you like chocolate mocha cream cake?" I asked. Oh dear, I just couldn't help myself with the questions, but no one liked an awkward silence.

He lifted the camera that was around his neck and took a picture of me.

I blinked at the dazzling flash. "You're into photography?"

Bruce sniffed the cake again. "Is this poisoned?"

I sucked in a breath. "No! Of course not. Why would you think that?"

"Where did it come from?"

"I made it. I'm Holly Holmes. I work at Audley Castle in the kitchen."

"You didn't leave the cakes unsupervised at any point? It would have been easy for someone to contaminate them."

"I know exactly what went in them. Why would you think they contain poison?"

"Because you could be one of them."

"One of them what?"

He glanced over his shoulder. "You need to be careful. They're always watching. They're always checking up on us and making sure we keep quiet."

"Who do you mean? And why do you need to keep quiet?" Bruce's pupils were dilated. Could he have taken something before the party?

He pressed a finger to his lips. "You need to keep your voice low. This place is bugged."

I glanced around the room. "Who do you think is bugging the manor house?"

"The ones who need the secrets kept. You shouldn't have come here with your poisoned cake. It's not safe." His hands shook as he lifted his camera again.

"Bruce, are you feeling okay? You look a bit shaky."

He tugged on the collar of his dirty shirt. "I need to do some recording."

"Oh! What are you recording?"

"Everything." He grabbed his camera and took several shots around the room. "I can't afford to miss anything. I left my camcorder in the bedroom. What if it gets tampered with?"

"I'm sure it's safe. Isn't everyone here your friend? They wouldn't tamper with your things."

Bruce sniffed the cake again before dropping it on the floor. "You don't understand. Nobody does." He turned and raced out of the room.

I stared after him. That was possibly the strangest conversation I'd ever had.

"Try not to take offense over Bruce's behavior." An older guy who looked to be in his early sixties strolled over. He picked up the dropped cake in a napkin and placed it on the table. "He doesn't mean any harm. I'm Clive Carrell." He held out his hand, and I shook it.

"Nice to meet you. I'm Holly. I'm not offended, but I am worried. Bruce was acting oddly."

"He hasn't been himself for a long time. I've known him since he was five years old and his family moved to Appledore. It's where I'm from. I only moved here recently for work."

"Has he always been … eccentric?"

"It's a kind way of putting it. No, Bruce was a normal kid. Very bright. He showed a lot of promise. He was friends with my daughter, and they were at the same school. He got in on a scholarship, I believe. He could ace any test, but he excelled in science."

I glanced at the door Bruce had fled through. "I remember where I've seen him. He spends a lot of time in the churchyard. I've never spoken to him. I figured he was the caretaker."

"No, he doesn't work at the church. I think he lives there," Clive said.

"He's homeless?"

"Bruce calls the churchyard his home. I get the impression he feels safe there."

"Aren't his parents around? Is there no one who can give him a place to stay?"

"His parents died five years ago in a boating accident. He took it hard. I mean, it would have upset anyone, but Bruce has always been sensitive."

"It's strange. The way he was talking, it made me wonder if he was under some kind of threat. He asked if the cake was poisoned and then said the room was bugged."

Clive sighed. "I'm not certain of his diagnosis, but Bruce has had mental health problems for the best part of a decade. As he gets older, things get worse. I don't know the details, but he's on strong medication, which can give him hallucinations. The meds make him paranoid."

"That's so sad. It sounds like he had a promising future when he was younger."

"He did. No one could keep up with Bruce in class. He even used to tutor Jacob in science and math. That's how they got to know each other. He was a brilliant kid, but his instability got the better of him. Such a waste." Clive shook his head and took a sip of his champagne.

"Is there a homeless shelter he can go to? Maybe he could get extra help?"

"There's nothing like that nearby. The closest is in Cambridge. Sir Richard is great and looks out for Bruce when he can. He even had an old barn cleared out so Bruce could live there after he moved from Appledore. It's got heat and power and a place for him to sleep. I think he uses it sometimes, but he prefers the churchyard."

"At least his friends haven't abandoned him. That's more than a lot of people would do."

"Jacob's a good kid. He takes after his father. They always look out for people who need help. There's Jacob coming in now." Clive beckoned Jacob Marchwood over. He was a classically good-looking guy, tall, broad-shouldered, with dark hair that he wore long to his collar.

Jacob smiled broadly at me. "Dad told me he's been upping the numbers for the party."

"I'm so sorry if you think I'm intruding," I said. "I was only here to deliver the cakes, but I had my arm twisted to stay."

"You're welcome, Holly. You always spoil us with delicious treats. It's one of the bonuses of moving to Audley St. Mary. And Meatball is making people smile, too."

I glanced over. Meatball was sitting on a guy's lap and wagging his tail.

"Actually, I'm happy to have a friendly face here." Jacob looked around the room. "I'm letting down the Marchwood reputation by not having a crazy time."

I glanced at Clive, not certain where he fit into the party dynamics. "These are all your old school friends?"

"Most of them are here from the old gang," Jacob said. "Clive's representing his daughter."

"Is she away somewhere?" I said to Clive.

Clive's gaze dipped. "I wish it was that simple. Unfortunately, Eleanor died."

I gasped, and my hand flew to my mouth. "I'm so sorry. That was tactless of me. I didn't even stop to think. Of course, why would you represent her if she was still alive?"

He lifted a hand and waved it slightly. "Eleanor died a long time ago. When I heard about the school reunion Jacob was putting together, I thought it might be nice to drop by, hear a few stories about her. Don't worry, I'll get out of the way when you young ones get rowdy."

"You're welcome to stay the whole evening, Mr. Carrell," Jacob said. "I'm sure Eleanor would have appreciated you being here. She was such a great girl. I still miss her."

"As do I. Every day." Clive set his glass down. "If you'll excuse me, I'm going to get some air."

"I feel terrible," I said once Clive had gone. "I had no idea about his daughter."

"Why would you? It happened over in Appledore. He doesn't talk about it much. Clive's a great guy. Dad has him working part-time on the estate as the handyman. He's a part of the furniture. He came with us when Dad moved."

"Do you know what happened to his daughter?"

Jacob's mouth twisted to the side. "Unfortunately, I do. We used to hang out together. She even dated Adam Remus for a while, although it wasn't anything serious. The best way to describe Eleanor was flighty. She'd get really excited about something one minute and forget it the next. We used to tease her about her short attention span.

We didn't realize she wasn't doing so well and her behavior was hiding a serious problem."

"She wasn't well?"

"Oh, no. I didn't mean she had an illness. Not a physical one, anyway. Things went wrong when Adam dumped her. You know what teenage boys are like. Selfish and self-obsessed. Adam thought things were getting too serious, so they split up. Eleanor spiraled. She went into this deep depression. We tried to cheer her up, tell her she'd find someone else, but she shut herself off. And then … well, she killed herself."

I squeezed my eyes shut for a second. "Now I feel even worse. I've ruined Clive's evening by reminding him what happened to his daughter."

"Clive will be okay. It did happen a long time ago. Eleanor was seventeen, so it was almost ten years ago. Of course, it hit him hard, but there was nothing anyone could have done to stop her. Eleanor was always fragile."

"Is her old boyfriend here tonight?" I asked.

"Yes, that's Adam over there." Jacob pointed to a short, stocky guy with dark hair and a gleaming smile. "I'll introduce you if you like."

"Actually, I wonder if I might steal Holly away." Rupert appeared by my side, holding two glasses of champagne.

"Of course," Jacob said. "You must know each other from the castle."

"I know Holly very well," Rupert said.

Jacob's eyebrows rose. He glanced from Rupert to me. "I see. Excellent choice."

"Excellent choice?" I said.

Jacob grinned. "If you'll excuse me, I'm neglecting the other partygoers. Enjoy your evening." He walked away.

I looked around the room. It really wasn't much of a party, and I wasn't doing anything to liven it up. So far, I'd talked about a girl's suicide and upset a homeless guy. "I should make a move. I seem to keep putting my foot in it tonight."

"You absolutely shouldn't leave. We've barely spent any time together. I never get you on your own. Alice always monopolizes your time." Rupert handed me a glass.

I glanced at him and my cheeks grew warm. He did look dashing. "Meatball seems to be having fun, so it isn't fair to leave right away and spoil his enjoyment. I can spare half an hour before I have to get back."

"I insist upon it. Come with me. I'll give you the grand tour."

With my hand tucked neatly in Rupert's crooked elbow, I happily let myself indulge in the fantasy of being lady of the manor house, even if it was just for a few minutes.

Chapter 3

"This staircase was designed by Montague Assiz over three hundred years ago." Rupert pointed out the expensive solid wood spindles.

"I'm impressed. The whole house is beautiful." Rupert had been showing me around for the last half an hour. So far, we'd seen a library that almost rivaled Audley Castle's, an entertainment room, a formal dining room, and several galleries set aside for Sir Richard's vast art collection.

"Would you like to live somewhere like this?" Rupert asked.

"I really haven't thought about it. I love my apartment in the grounds of the castle. It's all I need. I'd just rattle around if I had all these rooms. What would Meatball and I do with so much space?"

"You could set up a playroom just for Meatball," Rupert said. "Or you could hold parties like Sir Richard."

"I'm more of a homebody than a partygoer. Although I can always be tempted with a cup of tea and a nice slice of cake."

"Especially if it's your cake," Rupert said. "But what happens when your family gets larger?"

"You think I should get more dogs?"

He chuckled. "I was actually thinking about what will happen when you marry and have children. You'll soon outgrow your apartment."

A warmth spread up my neck. "Oh, I'm not sure that's for me. I mean, I like children, but I also love my work."

"You could have both. I had several wonderful nannies when I was a child."

"Your circumstances are different to mine, though. Besides, I wouldn't want a nanny to raise my children."

"It was fun. Alice and I had a great time. Our parents were always traveling, even back then, so we needed the stability of a nanny."

"You must miss your parents. When was the last time you saw them?"

"It must be six months ago. They have a lot of charity commitments. It takes them all over the world. And they're always being invited to different social events. It's important that they're seen in the right places with the right people."

"I'd have thought their children were the right people to be seen with most of the time."

He adjusted his tie. "I'm used to it. I really don't mind. And I always had Alice and the nanny to keep me entertained when I was younger. And now, I have you."

"I'm your entertainment?"

"No! I didn't mean that. I simply meant ... well, you're excellent company. I enjoy spending time with you."

"Likewise. I consider you a good friend."

"Ah, yes, friends. Of course. That's always a nice place to start."

It was a nice place to start and to stay. Anything more with Rupert, and I'd be in big trouble, no matter how cute I considered him in that suit.

We turned a corner and almost walked into an enormous guy with a short neck and huge arm muscles, dressed in a black suit. He had sunglasses on, even though he was inside.

"This area is out of bounds," he said.

"I'm just showing Holly round," Rupert said. "I'm sure Jacob won't mind if we take a peek in these rooms."

"I must insist you explore another part of the house," the man said. "These are the private family rooms."

I squeezed Rupert's elbow. "It's okay. I've seen enough. I do need to leave. We've got twelve coaches of tourists coming to the castle tomorrow afternoon. They'll all need feeding, which means extra work for me."

Rupert looked momentarily perplexed. "Are you sure?"

I gently tugged him away from the scowling security guard. "Certain."

Rupert frowned as we walked back along the corridor. "That security guy could have let us take a peek. It's not as if we were going to steal from the family."

"He was only doing his job. I'm surprised you don't have any castle security with you. They usually don't let you out of their sight."

"Campbell's around here somewhere. You know how good he is at lurking in the shadows so no one sees him."

I glanced around and dropped my hold on Rupert's elbow. Campbell Milligan always made snarky comments whenever I spent any time with Rupert.

We headed back the way we'd come, along a corridor and down a flight of stairs.

"Do you know Clive Carrell?" I said.

"Not really. I understand he works for Sir Richard. He was here tonight."

"And I ruined his mood. I put my foot in it when I made a comment about his daughter. I didn't realize she was dead," I said.

Rupert rubbed his chin. "You must mean Eleanor."

"That's right. Did you know her?"

"Not really. Jacob and his friends are a couple of years younger than me. I know of her, though. And I heard what happened."

"It was a suicide. That's so sad."

"That's what everyone says."

I glanced at him, noting the doubt in his tone. "You think different?"

"You hear a lot of things in a small place like this, but I did hear an odd rumor about a big cover-up."

"What kind of cover-up? Surely, if anything suspicious was discovered when she died, the police would have been involved."

"I've only ever heard second-hand accounts of what happened. But apparently, Eleanor was really into aliens."

My jaw dropped. "You mean, little green men?"

"All of that. She loved anything conspiracy related. The others were the same."

"The others?"

"Everyone here tonight. Eleanor was the most obsessed with aliens, though. She used to explore abandoned sites that were old government testing facilities, or something weird like that."

"She was hunting for aliens?"

"Or their spaceships, or whatever they used to travel in."

I laughed out loud. "You're teasing me. There's no such thing as secret government bunkers full of alien technology."

"I'm only telling you what I heard."

"Who told you this?"

"Take a guess. We do have an amazing source of gossip in the castle."

"Betsy Malone! It's got to be."

He grinned. "You got me."

"Betsy believes in UFOs?"

"Of course! She's over in Nevada as we speak, exploring Area 51 and getting her photo taken with ET."

"Now I know you're teasing. Betsy's gone to Disneyland in Paris. She talked of nothing else for weeks before she went."

"Maybe I am teasing a little. But there really was a rumor that Eleanor uncovered something big. The government got involved and killed her to keep her quiet. They made her death look like a suicide."

"That doesn't happen. Do you really believe that?"

He shook his head and grinned. "I don't, but I wanted to see your expression. I know you love a good mystery. I think it was a case of a vulnerable girl who took things too far."

"Jacob mentioned she used to date someone called Adam. When they split up, she didn't handle things too well."

"Yes, that's the real reason. Adam was really cut up about it. From what I remember, he went off the rails for a while. He was drinking too much, and possibly into drugs, although that was never confirmed. After Eleanor's suicide, the old gang fell apart."

"You know, it's not polite to gossip about the dead."

I gasped as a man in his late twenties stepped out of the shadows. He wore a pale gray suit with a blue shirt that was open at the neck, and a loose tie. He had a large glass of whiskey in one hand.

"Dexter, you gave us a fright," Rupert said. "Dexter Dubois, meet Holly Holmes."

I shook hands with him. "Sorry about the gossiping. That was my fault. I got curious when I met Clive and heard what happened to Eleanor. I didn't mean any disrespect."

He lifted one shoulder. "I was only teasing. And I expect Eleanor would be thrilled that people are talking about her attempts to uncover the secrets held by this fine country." He joined us as we continued walking along the corridor.

"She really was into the conspiracy stuff?" I asked.

"Eleanor loved it. She was always researching archives and trying to get her hands on government paperwork. Of course, there was nothing to find. She spent hours sifting through boring minutes of committee meetings and reading blogs written by other conspiracy theorists."

"She never found anything?" I said. "Some conspiracy theories out there are convincing. I heard about one where animals were trained to be spies. I think eagles were used to fly into other territory and see what the enemy was doing."

"At least you don't believe that the government is run by aliens," Dexter said.

"Oh! No. Is that what Eleanor thought?"

"Not really. Although she often talked about it in the gang."

"The gang? You were interested in conspiracy theories too?"

"No. I was interested in pretty girls and the fact Adam could always get his hands on free booze. That was tempting enough to go on the weird outings."

"Where did you go?" I said.

"We mainly stuck to local places. There were a few disused army bases Eleanor was obsessed with. She was always poking around them."

"I imagine those places are off-limits to the public."

"Yes, but if they've been out of action for fifty years, there are easy ways to get in, and you can always climb over the fence if you're careful. Most of them aren't even monitored anymore. Wherever we visited, Eleanor found something she thought was a clue to a cover-up. She once claimed she found an underground site used to hold prisoners of war."

"Which war?" I said.

Dexter laughed his strong-scented whiskey breath over me. "You sound like Eleanor. She was always trying to find an angle. She was just a pretty girl with a big imagination. I wish I'd paid her more attention. I reckon she was trying to find something weird or unusual so people would take notice of her."

"I met Clive. He seemed like a nice guy. Did they have a good relationship?" I asked.

"The best. She was a real daddy's girl. Her mom died when she was young, and I think she got lonely. I sometimes wonder if that was why she was always seeking attention, jumping from one thing to the other, trying to impress us. She needn't have bothered. She was a gorgeous girl with a great set of ..." He lifted his hands, and his gaze flashed to me. "I mean, she had beautiful eyes."

Rupert cleared his throat. "I believe several members of the original group couldn't be here tonight. Is that right?"

"Yes, Emily Smithers and Simone Matthews. I hoped to catch up with them. It's been ages since I've spoken to them. Emily's a psychiatrist. She's always busy. I read her latest paper online. Most of it went over my head."

"Maybe she couldn't get away from work," I said.

"Jacob sent her several messages and tried to phone her dozens of times, but she never got back to him. Then last week, she sent him a one-line message saying she was busy. That was it. No, how are you? Sorry, I can't make it. It was weird. Emily never used to be like that. She was always the warm, friendly one. She'd always bring new people into the gang."

"What about Simone?" I said.

Dexter took a sip of whiskey, a soft smile on his face. "Simone was a whole heap of fun. She was the wild one. That's another weird thing. No one's seen her since Eleanor died."

"She left Appledore? Did her parents move away?" I said.

"No, I mean, she vanished. She was close to Eleanor. Simone was from out of town. She was raised by a single mom, and they were always moving around. Appledore was the first place they settled." Dexter whistled. "Simone was out of this world gorgeous. She had raven hair and these brilliant blue eyes. Whenever she looked at you, it was like she was seeing right through you. She drew attention wherever she went. She could be in baggy jeans and a baseball cap, and people noticed her."

"What happened to her?" I said.

"I think she went abroad. The police even looked into it but didn't find anything suspicious. It was tricky, Simone was slightly older than us, almost eighteen when she left the village. Her mom asked around, but no one had seen her. Then she got a message to say where she was, and everything calmed down."

"You make it sound like she fell off the face of the earth," Rupert said.

"Jacob reckons she went to America," Dexter said.

"Do you think she met someone?" I said. "Maybe she ran away with them."

"There was no one special that I knew of, but Simone was always out and about with others. She was in our gang, but she was always the social butterfly."

"How many of you were in this gang?" I said.

Dexter grinned. "I like to call it a gang, but it was more of a weirdos club. I was in it, so were Adam and Eleanor, Emily, Simone, and Bruce."

"And you used to hunt down these conspiracies," Rupert said.

"Yep, that's pretty much what we did. And the occasional illicit drinking session and make out opportunity in the woods when the girls would let us. That definitely didn't happen as much as I liked."

"And you never found anything that convinced you about a conspiracy theory? Eleanor's hunt for aliens wasn't successful?" I said.

Dexter stopped walking. He glanced around, then leaned closer, a gleam of amusement in his eyes. "Have you ever heard of Octopus Labs?"

"Is that a local company?" I asked.

"Local enough. They used to run a laboratory over in Appledore."

"I've heard of them," Rupert said. "Did you find something there?"

"Eleanor thought something strange was going on there." Dexter grinned.

"Did you go and take a look?" I asked.

"It was the last place Eleanor was really interested in. She kept on talking about it. She dragged us out there a couple of times, but I wasn't impressed. It was a strange place. There was always a lot of security about."

"What were they protecting?" I asked.

"Alien spaceships," Rupert whispered, a grin on his face.

The door to our right opened. Adam poked his head out. "There you are, Dexter. Come on, I need you to settle a debate."

Dexter raised a hand. "I'll be right there." He turned to us. "Nice to meet you, Holly. Don't listen to any of my nonsense about conspiracy theories. Nothing exciting ever goes on in Appledore." He strolled away and into the room.

Rupert shook his head. "He almost had me convinced Eleanor found something alien at that site."

"Me, too. I think he was only playing with us, though." I continued walking along beside Rupert as he pointed out the carved cornicing, but my thoughts were elsewhere.

All this conspiracy theory business sounded far-fetched. Eleanor's suicide, Simone going missing, and some mysterious lab.

Was there more to Eleanor's death than everyone realized?

I shook my head. No, there couldn't be. It was simply my over-active imagination forcing the puzzle pieces into holes they didn't belong in. There was no mystery at Marchwood Manor.

Chapter 4

"I'm so glad you came here tonight." Rupert led me out the main front door, Meatball walking in between us, looking content at his unexpected role as entertainer for the night.

"Me, too. I've had a great evening. It was a treat seeing Marchwood Manor and spending time with you."

"I enjoyed it too," Rupert said. "We'll have to do it again, just the two of us."

This felt like it was straying close to date territory. In fact, the whole evening had felt like that, ever since I'd seen Rupert in the kitchen. I was fond of him, but I was also very fond of my job, my apartment, and my simple life. Getting involved with a lord who'd be in charge of Audley Castle one day was a whole level of complicated I wasn't ready to face.

"How about I think up a few ideas for our next adventure?" he said.

"We should investigate the mysterious lab Eleanor was interested in," I said. "See if the rumors are true."

"Oh, I was thinking of something a bit more romantic."

"Romantic!" My cheeks flamed. "Are you sure that's a good idea?"

"Maybe not. At least, something fun. There won't be much to see if we go to a disused building."

"I guess not."

Rupert stepped closer. He touched my arm, and a warmth spread through me as I looked into his blue eyes. If only he wasn't so nice. If only he wasn't so handsome. If only he wasn't a lord.

My eyes widened. Was he going to kiss me? He was leaning closer, inching toward me.

The front door was yanked open. Jacob and Dexter stumbled out, their arms around each other's shoulders.

"Oh, sorry! We didn't know anyone was out here." Jacob straightened, his eyes sparkling and his cheeks pink. He had a glass of champagne in one hand.

Dexter staggered to the side and caught hold of a pillar to stop from toppling over. "We didn't catch you two doing something you shouldn't, I hope."

Rupert stepped back, his own cheeks bright pink. "Of course not. I was just making sure Holly got into the van safely."

"She won't come to any harm out here," Jacob said. "Come on, Dexter. Let's leave these two lovebirds to it."

"It's not like that," I said. "We're just ... friends." I heard the lie as I said it.

Rupert glanced away, but I didn't miss the flash of hurt on his face. What did he expect me to say? He was probably going to marry some princess from an Icelandic country. He could never marry a kitchen assistant. Besides, maybe this kitchen assistant wasn't the marrying kind.

"We'll go around the side," Jacob said. "Rupert, I've got a spare cigar if you want a smoke."

"No, thanks," Rupert said.

"Your loss. They're Havana cigars. Specially imported." Jacob waggled a long thick cigar at him.

"Thanks. I'll pass," Rupert said.

"While you're here, take a look at this." Dexter struggled to get his cell phone out of his jacket pocket. "We're getting a group together for a winter ski vacation. You've been on the Alps a few times. Where's the best spot?"

Rupert glanced at me. "Um, well, there are several."

"You go. I'll be fine. I need to get Meatball home and in bed, or he'll be grumpy in the morning." I gave him a reassuring smile.

"I'm sorry about this," Rupert said. "We were having such a pleasant evening."

"And it's still pleasant. I'll see you tomorrow." I hurried away before I said or did something I may regret.

I'd just buckled Meatball securely into the passenger seat of the van, when the hairs on the back of my neck prickled. I turned to discover Campbell Milligan standing a foot away from me.

"Doing your usual scary lurking, I see." I shut the passenger door.

"And you're doing your usual flirting with someone you shouldn't," he said.

"I didn't know you had an interest in my love life."

"I have an interest in anything a member of the Audley family does."

"Well, as you'd have observed all evening, nothing inappropriate happened. I simply kept Lord Rupert company while we looked round Marchwood Manor."

"You were almost holding hands at one point."

I scowled at him. "That's not true. Maybe you need to get your eyes checked. You can't make mistakes on the job."

"You be careful mixing with the rich and famous," Campbell said.

"That almost sounds like a threat."

"It's a friendly warning. Their lives are so much more complicated than ours."

"I imagine your life must be pretty complicated. After all, you're always having to figure out how to hide in plain sight and sneak around scaring the life out of people for no reason."

He shot me a shark-like grin. "Do I scare you, Holmes?"

"Only about once a day. And I'm getting used to it." I walked to the other side of the van.

Campbell followed me.

"Was there something you needed?" I asked.

"I want to make sure you get safely off the premises. I don't want Lord Rupert coming back and twisting your arm to stay."

"I'm going. I won't get in your way." I was about to get in the van but turned back. "Actually, you might be able to help me with something."

"If you're lost, you go straight along the gravel drive and turn right."

"I know my way home, wise guy."

He shrugged. "What do you need?"

"I was talking to some guests at the party tonight. Have you ever heard of Eleanor Carrell?"

"I know Clive Carrell. Are they related?"

"She was his daughter. She died ten years ago. Apparently, it was a suicide."

Campbell's forehead furrowed. "I wasn't around ten years ago. I'm not familiar with that case. What has she got to do with the castle?"

"Nothing. It's just that it's all a bit strange. She killed herself after her boyfriend, Adam Remus, dumped her."

"And?"

"And nothing. She was really into alien conspiracy theories. Just before she died, she was looking at an old testing lab in Appledore."

"And?"

I tutted. "Stop doing that. It's annoying."

"I aim to please. Why are you poking at a ten-year-old suicide?"

I chewed on my bottom lip. "It seems a bit of a coincidence that she was into conspiracy theories, started a new investigation, and then died."

"It was a suicide. There's no mystery here."

"Yes, but what if it wasn't? What if she found out something she shouldn't?"

"Is that overactive imagination of yours misbehaving?"

"Probably. I just … I don't know. Something seems a bit off here."

His smile faded. "How old was she when she died?"

"Seventeen."

"You think a seventeen-year-old girl uncovered some big alien conspiracy theory and got bumped off because of it?"

"Well, it's possible."

"If you're writing a Hollywood movie script."

"Have you really not heard about her?"

He sighed. "I've heard a couple of things. Only thirdhand information, which I don't pay attention to." His lips thinned, and he crossed his arms over his chest.

"You could always ask the security here. They're as strict as you. We got stopped from exploring by a giant of a man in sunglasses."

Campbell snorted. "No chance. The security team is reluctant to share any information."

"Don't you get along? The guy we met was on the abrupt side. All you security types are the same."

"I'm nothing like that jerk."

I leaned closer. "I smell a story."

"Then you need to blow your nose."

"Campbell, come on. Is there rivalry between Audley Castle and Marchwood Manor? Who was the rude guy in the shades?"

Campbell sucked air between his teeth. "Lee Mahoney. He runs the security for Sir Richard."

"From the sour look on your face, you two aren't friends."

"Let's say we have a difference of opinion over most things."

"Like what?"

He stiffened, and his gaze moved over my head. "Perfect. It's like he knows he's being talked about."

I turned to see Lee approaching. He had the swagger of someone who was carrying something wedged under his armpits, so his arms stuck out.

"What are you doing out here, Campbell?" Lee strode over, his sunglasses still in place. "You should be guarding your mark, not chatting up this piece of skirt."

"Have some respect, Mahoney. Lord Rupert Audley is just round the corner."

"Yes, have some respect. I'm not a piece of skirt," I said.

Lee lowered his shades. His cold blue gaze ran over me, his eyes lingering on my chest for an inappropriate amount of time, before he grunted and shoved the shades back up his nose.

"I work with Holly," Campbell said. "Not that it's any of your business."

Lee smirked. "You're standing close for work colleagues. What does she do for you?"

"Are you looking for a smack?" Campbell practically growled the words.

I smiled brightly at Lee. Perhaps a charm offensive was needed, or at least a distraction, before these two came to blows. "Were you employed by the Marchwoods when Eleanor Carrell died?"

He looked at me but didn't answer.

Campbell growled again, low in his chest. "You won't get anything out of him, Holly."

"I don't have to answer questions from either of you," Lee said. "Besides, that's ancient news. It's also none of your business."

He was a charmer. "I never said it was. I was just curious after hearing about Eleanor."

"Don't be. Curiosity gets people in trouble. The dead kind of trouble."

I blinked at him. "I, um, well, I guess it does if you ask the wrong questions."

"You should take her home," Lee said to Campbell.

"I can take myself home, thanks very much," I said.

"She can," Campbell said. "And that's what she was doing."

I gritted my teeth. Two alpha males were so frustrating to be around. Still, I couldn't resist prodding. "It's a pity neither of you know what went on with Eleanor. Surely, two such knowledgeable gentlemen would have their eye on the ball when it came to all things related to these families. After all, your primary purpose is to keep them safe."

"Watch it, Holly," Campbell said.

I flashed Lee a smile. "I'm sure you know all about what happened, you just don't like to share."

"The death of some kid a decade ago has nothing to do with me," Lee said. "A dumb girl drinks too much and has her heart broken because some horny teenage boy won't put a ring on her finger. Not my problem. Not the family's problem."

"So you do know about Eleanor," I said.

Campbell smirked. "You need to watch out for Holly. She never misses a trick."

"Then she won't miss this trick. Get out of here," Lee said. "You're not on the official guest list."

"Maybe not. But I had a personal invite from Sir Richard. I can stay if I want to." I lifted my chin, refusing to be bullied by this overly muscled meathead.

"You don't want to stay. You were just leaving," Campbell said.

"That's it. You keep your girlfriend in line, Campbell." Lee smirked again, then turned and strode away.

"Wow! I thought you were mean. He's an A Grade jerk," I said.

"He absolutely is," Campbell said. "I can't stand the guy."

"What's his background? Something must have happened to make him turn so mean."

Campbell was silent.

"I absolutely know you'd have looked into his background. Is he former military, like you?"

"Something like that. He's also ex-police. He reckons he's the next James Bond."

"He's got the build for it. Although he looks too pumped up to be Bond. Bond is always leanly muscled. Lithe, like an athlete."

Campbell shook his head. "Weren't you leaving?"

"I'm out of here." I looked around. "I just want to say goodbye to Lord Rupert."

"He won't miss you leaving. Get out of here, Holmes, before you start any more trouble."

"I was on my best behavior tonight. You were the one trying to start a fight with 007."

Campbell strode over and yanked open the van door.

"Oh, there's Rupert. Give me a minute, I'll go and see him." I ignored Campbell's sigh as I dashed away from the van.

I lifted a hand and waved at Rupert, turning as I heard someone cry out.

I screamed as two solid arms wrapped around me and I was thrown to the ground. I rolled over several times before coming to land on my back in the gravel. Campbell was lying on top of me.

"What did you do that for? I only wanted to say goodbye?" I tried to wriggle out from under Campbell.

"Don't move."

A second later, there was a ground-jarring thud close to my head.

Campbell leaped off me and turned.

I rolled onto my hands and knees, dazed and confused. The breath whooshed from my lungs as I took in the scene.

Where I'd been standing, there was a body on the ground.

I scrambled over, barely noticing the cuts on my hands from the gravel.

Campbell leaned over the body. "It's Adam Remus."

"Is he ..." My gaze went up into the gloom, where he must have plummeted from.

"Oh yes," Campbell said. "He's one hundred percent dead."

Chapter 5

I was inching toward Adam's body, my insides shaking and my stomach rolling over, when there was an angry yell.

"Get away from there. You'll mess with the scene." Lee raced over, a scowl on his face.

Campbell straightened from his inspection of the body and glared at him. "I was checking to see if he was alive."

"You moron. No one survives a fall from that height." Lee shoved Campbell back. "This isn't your security detail. Butt out."

"I'm glad it isn't, since you've got a dead guy to deal with." Campbell stepped into Lee's personal space.

"Um, shouldn't we be more concerned about the man lying dead on the ground than who's the biggest alpha around here?" I got to my feet, my knees shaky.

Lee grunted. "Both of you need to move along."

Campbell remained firmly planted where he was. He spread his legs and puffed out his chest. "Shouldn't you check where he fell from?"

"I plan to." Lee glared back at him.

Neither of them moved.

I cleared my throat. This situation needed a level head, not a scowling one. "Have either of you thought that this wasn't an accident? There could be a killer on the roof you need to stop."

Campbell flicked me a glance. "Holly has a point."

Lee ran his tongue across his teeth. "Even if she does, you still need to leave. I'll have my team check over everything. You don't need to tell me my job."

"Someone should," Campbell said.

Jacob, Dexter, and Rupert strolled around the side of the manor. They froze for a second as they took in the shocking scene.

"What the heck is going on here?" Jacob raced over with Dexter and Rupert. "Is that … Adam?"

"Sir, you don't need to see this." Lee moved to block his view. "There's been an accident."

Jacob looked at me, the color gone from his face. "Did you see what happened?"

"She's not important in this incident. I'll conduct a full investigation, sir," Lee said.

"He … he was my friend. I don't understand." Jacob's gaze shot to the roof of the manor house. "What was he doing up there?"

"You think he was on the roof?" I said.

Lee glared at me and leaned closer to Campbell. "Keep your girlfriend under control."

Campbell sucked in a deep breath.

I grabbed his arm and gave it a hard squeeze. "I'm just trying to help. How did Adam manage to get on the roof?"

"He wasn't on the roof. There's a wraparound veranda up there." Jacob's voice was shaky. "You can get out and view the grounds. I … I don't understand. Why would he go up there? You can't see anything in the middle of the night."

"Holly, are you okay?" Rupert moved to my side.

"It was a close call, but I'm fine. Actually, Campbell helped me."

Rupert turned his attention to Campbell. "You saved Holly?"

"She was standing under Adam when he fell," Campbell said. "She could have been injured. Anyone would have done the same."

As the realization sank in about how close to death I'd been, my body shook. I swayed from side to side. It was only Rupert catching me by the shoulders that stopped me going down.

"Let's get you out of here," he said. "You need something for the shock."

"It's best if everyone leaves, Lord Rupert," Lee said. "I need the scene cleared as quickly as possible."

Jacob raked a hand down his face before turning to Dexter. "We should go inside. Let Lee do his job. We'll have to contact Adam's family. What a terrible piece of news to deliver. Oh, what about the police?"

"I'll keep them informed," Lee said. "They're usually cooperative. They won't get in your way. They know your father has an expert team in place to deal with matters like this."

"Of course. Thanks, Lee." Jacob shook his head, his gaze on the body. "The poor guy. I invited him here for a fun weekend and this happens." He looked up at the roof again, then walked away with Dexter.

"We should go too, Holly," Rupert said softly. "You've gone very pale. You need a brandy."

I had a dozen questions in my head, but none would settle. I glanced at Campbell, who was glaring at Lee, before being led away by Rupert.

When I got to the van, Meatball had his nose pressed to the glass, panic in his dark eyes.

I scooped him out and hugged him. What a terrible night. All I'd planned to do was make a quick delivery, and I ended up almost being squashed by a falling person. That would teach me not to gate crash a party ever again.

❦

"I still can't believe a man almost fell on your head last night." Gran fussed around me, pouring out more tea and insisting I tell her the tale of what happened at Marchwood Manor again.

"I'm still in shock. If Campbell hadn't shoved me out the way, there would have been two bodies to deal with," I said.

Gran's hand fluttered on her chest. "Don't say that. I'm not a big Campbell fan, but he really came through. All those muscles are good for something." She settled in the seat opposite me and poured her own mug of tea.

Saffron jumped onto her lap and snuggled down.

"He did. I'll have to bake him something delicious to say thank you."

"Do you know anything about the man who died?"

"Not much. His name was Adam Remus. I didn't get a chance to talk to him at the party. He was a school friend of Jacob Marchwood."

Gran nodded. "And it was definitely an accident?"

"I don't have a clue. There was a lot of alcohol flowing at the party. I guess Adam could have stumbled and fallen over the ledge. I've never been up on the veranda, though. Lee Mahoney runs the security for the Marchwood family, and he gave nothing away. He even told Campbell to butt out." I sipped my tea. "It was a strange evening. It was nice spending time with Rupert, but I heard about one of the group members who killed herself ten years ago. They were all part of some conspiracy gang and went around looking for aliens and government cover-ups."

"That's not a healthy hobby for a young woman."

"The whole thing sounded odd. Her name was Eleanor Carrell. She was looking into some old testing facility just before she died. And I was wondering—"

"You were wondering if there was more to her death than suicide." Gran shook her head, her eyes sparkling. "You never could resist a mystery. That would be a cold case, though. And surely if anything strange happened to her, the police would have investigated. I imagine it's hard to fake suicide."

"I've never really thought about it."

"You shouldn't. And I think you should take the day off work after the shock you've had."

"I'm glad I've got the morning off, thanks to my late-night baking adventures," I said. "I do feel a little wobbly. And I didn't sleep well."

"That's no surprise. I'll tell Chef Heston you won't be in all day."

I grabbed her arm before she could move. "Don't do that. He won't be happy, and we're really busy this afternoon. I'm fine. I'll take Meatball for a long walk to clear my head. That always makes me feel better."

Gran pursed her lips, and her gaze ran over me. "You're not fine. You saw a dead body last night. And that body almost killed you. You're my favorite granddaughter—I can't have anything like that happening."

I laughed. "I'm your only granddaughter."

There was a knock on the front door. Meatball barked and raced over to it.

"You stay where you are." Gran stood and cupped Saffron in her arms. "I'll get that."

"It's probably the police here for my statement."

"I'll send them away if you're not up to seeing them." Gran headed to the door.

"No, I want to talk to them. I want to find out what happened."

Gran pulled open the door. "Oh! Hello, Ray."

"Good morning, Molly and Saffron. I hope it's not too early for you." He held out a large bunch of pink and white wildflowers. "I saw these and thought of you. Beautiful, a little wild, and one of a kind."

"You old charmer. They are beautiful. Are they from the garden?" Gran took the flowers and sniffed them.

"That's right. Fresh-cut this morning." He glanced in the door and spotted me. "Morning, Holly."

"Hi, Ray."

"Come in. I'll get you a coffee," Gran said. "We were having breakfast and talking over Holly's adventures last night. You're not going to believe what happened to her."

"Adventures?" Ray walked into the kitchen. "What have you been up to this time, Holly?"

Before I had a chance to answer, there was another knock on the front door.

"That'll be the police." Gran set the flowers in the sink and placed Saffron on the floor.

"The police!" Ray looked at me. "You've not got yourself in trouble, have you?"

"No, but trouble found me," I said.

Gran open the door to find Campbell standing outside. "I don't see any flowers."

Campbell's brow furrowed. "Flowers? You've lost me."

"It's good manners for gentleman callers to bring flowers." Gran pointed over her shoulder. "Ray knows how to treat a lady. You should have brought flowers for Holly."

Campbell looked momentarily bewildered. "I'll remember that for the next time." He looked past Gran. "I need to talk to Holly."

"She's not accepting visitors," Gran said. "She needs time to recover."

"Gran! I'm okay. Come in if you like, Campbell."

Meatball danced around Campbell's legs, then shot outside.

I jumped up from my seat. "On second thought, Meatball is overdue his walk. Have you eaten breakfast?" I asked Campbell.

"Just a protein shake before my workout."

I wrinkled my nose. "Yuck. That won't do. Give me a minute, I'll grab food and we can talk while I'm walking Meatball."

"Are you sure you're up to going out?" Gran followed me round the kitchen as I assembled a small hamper of breakfast scones, croissants, and fresh fruit.

"It'll do me good to get the facts together," I said. "Campbell was there last night. He saw what happened. Once I know what went on, I'll feel more settled."

"Just be careful. Don't get involved in something you shouldn't."

"I tell her that all the time." Campbell was still in the doorway. "She never listens to me."

Gran gave a snort of surprise. "Well, I suppose that's something we have in common. You make sure you keep Holly safe."

Campbell took a step back. "I'll wait outside until you're ready."

Five minutes later, I was buttoned up in my coat and out the door, Meatball racing ahead of me and Campbell.

"I didn't get a chance to thank you for saving my life." I handed him a filled ham and cheese croissant. "What made you shove me out the way?"

He bit into the croissant and chewed for a few seconds. "I heard a scuffling sound above us. I couldn't see what was going on because it was dark, but then I heard a yell."

"I heard that too. Did you see Adam fall?"

"I wasn't sure what I saw. Suddenly something large was flying through the air and heading straight for you."

"Well, I appreciate the shove out of the way." I looked at the small cuts on my hands from where I'd hit the ground. They were worth it. At least I was alive.

"I'm happy to shove you anytime, Holmes."

I selected a scone and bit into it. "Did you get a chance to look at the place Adam fell from?"

"No. Lee was being a jerk. He frogmarched me away from the manor house after you and Lord Rupert left and ordered me to leave. Lee said Marchwood Manor was his jurisdiction, and this was none of my business."

"I know you security experts take your jobs seriously, but he was on another level of rudeness."

"He's always been like that. He's also demanding statements from us but refuses to answer a single question from me."

"Hmmm, I know how that feels."

Campbell smirked. "I keep you out of the loop for your own good. You're not qualified to investigate crimes."

"And yet I seem to do okay when I do."

"You have your moments. Some might call them lucky breaks."

"Then let's hope my luck holds on this case." I finished my scone. "Why do you and Lee not get along?"

"Long story."

"We've got time. Meatball likes a long walk."

He finished his croissant and reached his hand out for another.

I handed him one. "I'm going to keep on asking questions. I'm guessing you have a history with Lee. You said he was in the police."

"Yup."

"Is that how you met?"

"Nope."

"Did you used to date?"

"Holly!"

"I told you, I'll keep digging until you cave."

"Fine. We know each other from our time in the military. Lee was discharged under dubious circumstances."

"What were those dubious circumstances?"

"Nothing was proven, but there were rumors of bullying and theft. He's not a nice guy. He always acts like he has something to prove."

"I know somebody else like that."

"I'm nothing like Lee. He thinks he knows everything and always has to be right."

There was so much I wanted to say to Campbell, but I stuffed a chunk of pineapple in my mouth, instead.

We walked in silence for a moment, enjoying the food and the fresh morning air. I was already feeling better.

"You know what we need to do?" I said.

"Find a way to make Lee Mahoney disappear for good?"

I choked out a laugh. "That's something I'm sure you could arrange."

"It wouldn't be difficult."

"We need to see the scene and find out exactly where Adam fell from."

"I tried to do that last night. Lee stopped me."

"Oh my goodness! There you are. I was worried about you." Princess Alice Audley raced over, her long blonde hair loose and her dress buttoned the wrong way.

"Why were you worried about me?" I said.

"I've just heard what happened last night from Rupert." She fluttered her eyelashes at Campbell. "Good morning, Campbell."

He nodded and wiped crumbs from his mouth. "Princess Alice."

"Why didn't you tell me the news last night when you got back from Marchwood Manor?" Alice grabbed my arm and tucked a hand through my elbow. "You always get to go to the exciting parties."

"Alice! Seeing a man fall to his death was hardly exciting. It was gruesome. There was blood. A lot of it."

"Eww! That is nasty." She wrinkled her nose. "Ooh! Is that a croissant I see in your hamper?"

I chuckled. "Yes. Would you like one?"

"Please. I'm starving. I only had fruit for breakfast and I'm already hungry. Plus, I abandoned my plate after Granny summoned me and made me even more stressed. That's something else I need to tell you. It's to do with the murder."

"Princess Alice, we're not sure it was murder," Campbell said. "It's early days in the investigation."

"It is." Alice tugged on my arm. "Holly, you must come with me immediately. Granny insists on seeing you."

I looked at Campbell. I really wanted to finish our conversation. "What's the emergency?"

She leaned closer until her mouth was by my ear. "Granny thinks you're dead. And she's seen a murder."

I jerked back. "She has? Not mine?"

"No, well, maybe." Alice glanced at Campbell. "There's no point in telling you about this. You never believe Granny and her premonitions. Holly, you must come with me. I order it."

"I should be heading over to my team." Campbell nodded at me. "We'll talk later."

"Let me know when Lee needs our statements," I said.

He grunted before striding away.

I turned my full attention to Alice. "What did Lady Philippa see? Does this have something to do with Adam?"

Alice jiggled on her toes, her blue eyes sparkling. "She saw the murder happen at Marchwood Manor. And you're involved."

Chapter 6

"Alice, has Lady Philippa seen me die?" I dashed along beside her to the castle.

"No! She's confused. I told her not to panic, but she insisted I find you. I knew you weren't dead after speaking to Rupert, but she wouldn't believe me," Alice said.

"Maybe we should have brought Campbell with us." I hurried to keep up with her as she skipped up the east turret stairs to Lady Philippa's rooms.

Meatball was ahead of her, never happy to brave the cold, creepy staircase.

"Any other time, I'd have been thrilled to have him around, but you know what Campbell's like when we talk about Granny's premonitions. He gets that weird look on his face as if he's constipated and starts muttering under his breath."

"If only her premonitions were clearer. Maybe we'd be able to stop a death, rather than pick up the pieces after the event has happened," I said.

"I'd prefer it if she didn't have them at all. The whole spooky business sends a shiver down my spine every time I think about it. And it took me ages to calm Granny down this morning and find out what was wrong. To begin with, she kept saying your name and that you were in trouble. She had me all panicked."

"It was a close call last night. Campbell really did save the day by pushing me out the way."

"I'm always telling you he's such a hero. You never believe me."

"I do in this instance."

Alice pushed open the main door that led into Lady Philippa's living room. "Granny, it's only us. I found Holly. She's not dead."

Lady Philippa raced to the door, dressed in a green silk, floor-length robe. She wrapped me in an enormous floral-scented hug and squeezed me so hard my ribs protested. "I was certain you'd died. I saw a man fall on your head."

I wriggled out of her embrace. "I'm very much alive."

She pinched my arm. "You're not a new addition to the castle ghosts. What a relief."

I rubbed the spot where she'd pinched me. "I'm fine. Alive and kicking."

"So, I got it wrong?" Lady Philippa tilted her head. "I never do that. No one died last night?"

"Oh, they did. Adam Remus almost landed on my head. It happened at Marchwood Manor," I said.

Lady Philippa clicked her fingers. "I knew it. Sit down, both of you. I've just had breakfast delivered, and there's plenty to go round. You must tell me everything." She hurried us to the table, and I settled in a seat.

"Thanks. I've already eaten," I said.

"At least have a cup of tea," Lady Philippa said. "Alice, you can pour."

"I'll do it." I reached for the teapot.

"You'll do no such thing. You almost died. You made my heart go all funny when I had that premonition," Lady Philippa said.

"Sorry to alarm you." I sat back and accepted a cup of tea from Alice.

"So, what happened to this dead man? What did you see?" Lady Philippa said.

"I went to Sir Richard's to deliver cake, and he invited me to his son's party that evening. I was reluctant, but Rupert was already there, so I stayed a while and had a look round. I was just leaving, when there was a yell and Adam hit the ground."

"Campbell saved Holly at the last second," Alice said. "He changed the future. If it wasn't for him, Holly really would be a castle ghost."

Lady Philippa leaned closer, the scone in her hand forgotten. "Who killed Adam?"

"I'm not sure anyone did. I couldn't get on the veranda to take a look. And Sir Richard's security wouldn't let Campbell anywhere near the scene. It could have been an accident."

"This was no accident." Lady Philippa placed her scone down. "Adam Remus was murdered."

Alice swatted the back of my hand. "This is much more interesting than some drunken fool toppling off the veranda and almost squashing you."

"It was a horrible shock for everyone who was there. Why do you think it was murder, Lady Philippa?"

"I saw it happen. Just before that young man fell, he was arguing with someone. Then it gets a bit strange. I saw him rushing toward you. I must have been looking through Adam's eyes as he fell." Lady Philippa drew in a deep breath and let it out slowly. "I've never done that before, inhabited a victim seconds before his death. My ability must be developing."

"We don't want that," Alice said. "It's creepy enough as it is. What else did you see?"

"That was it. I fainted because I was so shocked. I only woke when Horatio licked my face. We have to find out who killed that young man."

"I'm not sure it'll be that easy. I can't look at the scene, so I have no idea if anything bad happened to Adam."

"We'll see about that," Lady Philippa said. "I'm friends with Ricky Marchwood. He'll understand your interest, given you were almost the second victim in this heinous crime."

I twisted the cup in my hands. "There is something troubling me."

"Go on," Alice said. "I knew you wouldn't be able to resist this mystery."

"It's not so much about Adam. It's about another death."

"Two deaths! Who else died at the party?" Lady Philippa looked aghast.

"No one. But I was talking to some partygoers. I learned about Eleanor Carrell's suicide."

"Oh! I remember her," Lady Philippa said. "The poor girl was devastated after her beau left her."

"That's what I heard," I said. "Then I learned that everyone at the party was in a conspiracy group. They'd go around looking into alien cover-ups."

Alice gasped. "I love aliens. They're up there, just waiting for the right time to introduce themselves."

"Alice! You do talk nonsense," Lady Philippa said.

I grinned. "I don't believe they ever found an alien, but Dexter, who was at the party, mentioned Eleanor was investigating a disused government site in Appledore. It was called Octopus Labs."

"You mean the Octopus Group," Lady Philippa said.

"It's an odd name for a business. It could be the same place. Do you know what they did there?"

"It wasn't run by the government," Lady Philippa said. "It was a product testing facility for new food."

"Let me look them up." I pulled out my cell phone and did a search on the Internet. "You're right. Octopus Group was the fifth largest producer of quality control and testing for fine foods and beverages. With rigorous quality controls, you're guaranteed only excellence reaching the consumer."

"They probably tested everything from pork pies to pizza. No aliens would have been harmed in the testing of our food," Lady Philippa said.

"It could be a front for secret alien activities." Alice leaned forward in her seat. "Eleanor met one of the aliens and had to be silenced."

"That girl simply had her heart broken. Most of us get over something like that." Lady Philippa shook her head. "It's a tragedy, not an alien abduction."

I brought up pictures of the site. "Why does a product testing place need guards and high fences?" I showed them the pictures.

"To keep out the competition," Lady Philippa said. "A successful new product is big business. They'd probably get paid a percentage of the profits if it was a success."

"How do you know that, Granny?" Alice said.

"I may be an old woman confined to a castle turret, but I once had a life outside of these stone walls."

"All that barbed wire to protect their assets," I said. "It seems extreme. And in this picture, I see six guards. It looks like at least two of them have guns."

"To protect them in case the evil aliens escaped," Alice said.

"The corporate world is cutthroat," Lady Philippa said. "I'm not sure what this has to do with Eleanor's death. I can't imagine a group of teenagers would be interested in a food testing place."

"How about this for an idea? Maybe the octopus people secretly tested food on the group and something went wrong." Alice examined her waffle. "It could have made Eleanor sick, and they had to hush her up."

"Murdered over a slice of dodgy cheese. Not likely," Lady Philippa said. "They wouldn't have risked their reputation handing out the food they were testing."

I sipped my tea. "It was just a thought. Dexter brought it up, but he had been drinking a lot that night. The alcohol was seeping through his pores. Maybe he was joking around."

"Joking about a dead friend isn't amusing," Alice said.

"Most likely that group were simply bored and had nothing better to do. They had too much free time on their hands and let their imaginations run wild. Appledore isn't a hotbed of excitement for teenagers," Lady Philippa said.

I brought up a new search box and typed in *Eleanor Carrell* and *suicide*. There wasn't much information, a few old newspaper articles and some pictures.

"Holly, share your thoughts," Alice said. "Do you think Eleanor and Adam's deaths are connected?"

"I ... probably not." My gut twinged. "After all, Eleanor died a decade ago."

"Stick to the basics," Lady Philippa said. "I'm much more interested in Adam. Who was at the party last night?"

"There weren't many people," I said. "Most of us were outside when Adam fell."

"Or was pushed to his death by a human-alien hybrid determined to keep him silent," Alice said.

"Um, or that. I was outside with Campbell. Rupert was round the side of the manor house with Jacob and Dexter. I met Eleanor's father, Clive, but he left earlier in the evening." I tipped my head back. "That only leaves one person not accounted for."

"Could that person be the killer?" Alice said.

I bit my bottom lip. "Bruce Jonas. He was the first person I met at the party. He was a bit ... strange."

"Bruce? The man who spends most of his time in our churchyard?" Lady Philippa said. "He's young, very scruffy, but always polite. He often has a camera with him."

"That's him. I recognized him when we were introduced, but it took me a few minutes to place where I'd seen him. He lives in the churchyard most of the time."

"Why was he at the party?" Alice said.

"He went to school with Jacob and his friends. From what I was told, he was a clever guy and going places, but he has mental health problems. When we were talking, he kept saying strange things. He asked if my cake was poisoned, he said people were watching him, and he was convinced the room was bugged."

"He doesn't sound stable. Did you feel he was dangerous?" Alice said.

"No, he was just intense."

"Do you know where Bruce was when Adam was pushed?" Lady Philippa said.

"I've no idea. He raced away, saying he needed to get his camcorder from his room. He said he had to keep a record of things. That was at the start of the evening. I didn't see him after that."

"Well, there you are," Lady Philippa said. "This is an easy one for you to solve, Holly."

"You mean, this has nothing to do with aliens?" Alice's bottom lip jutted out.

"Slow down. Just because I don't know Bruce's alibi, it doesn't mean he killed Adam," I said. "We don't even know for certain Adam was killed."

"What does your gut tell you?" Alice said.

I blew out a breath. I'd had an uneasy feeling ever since Adam died. "That I should keep out of this."

"This is probably the easiest mystery you've ever been involved in. We know who killed Adam," Lady Philippa said.

"We do?"

"Bruce!" Lady Philippa nodded. "Now, we've solved that mystery, who wants a pancake?"

I shook my head as I sat back in my seat. Somehow, I didn't think this would be as simple as Lady Philippa thought.

The big question was, should I get involved?

Chapter 7

After my breakfast with Lady Philippa and Alice, I took Meatball for a walk around the grounds, my thoughts full of murder, government cover-ups, and mystery. Was I reading too much into what happened to Adam?

By the time I got back to my apartment, Gran had gone out.

I took a long shower, did a load of washing, and made a list of grocery items I needed.

I was glad I'd had the morning off work. Everything felt organized and back in its place. And if I didn't think about what happened at Marchwood Manor last night, I had nothing to worry about.

I checked the time, collected Meatball from his dog bed, and we left the apartment. I made the short walk to the kitchen, and after settling Meatball in his kennel, I pulled on my apron and got to work.

Chef Heston sidled over a few minutes later. "I heard there was an incident at Marchwood Manor."

I paused from stirring the chocolate mocha cake batter. "You mean Adam Remus?"

"If that's the chap who fell off the roof, then yes. How do you always manage to get yourself in the middle of these things?"

"Not by choice. I'd be much happier if a man hadn't tried to fall on my head. What have you heard?"

"The usual village gossip. The old ladies in the post office were talking about nothing else when I stopped by this morning."

"I'm not surprised. It was a shock."

"I hope it won't affect your work."

"Nothing ever affects my work. I was here on time, and I've already started my first task."

He inspected the contents of my bowl. "Well, if you need five minutes at any point, you let me know." He gave me a brief pat on my arm and walked away.

Chef Heston was bewildering. One second he was snapping, the next he was making sure I was doing okay.

"Excuse me. Have you got a minute, Holly?"

I turned to the kitchen door leading in from the yard. "Jacob! Of course. How are you? You must be feeling terrible after yesterday." I wiped my hands on a clean towel and hurried over to him.

Tiredness sat beneath his eyes and it looked like he hadn't shaved. "I don't feel great. I can't believe what happened."

"Neither can I. What can I do to help you?"

"I really came by to see how you were doing. After all, you had a near miss. Dad was insistent I check on you. I heard your security man saved you at the last second."

"He did. It's good of you both to think of me. Don't worry. I'm made of strong stuff. Seeing what happened to Adam was horrible, but I've got friends and family around me if I need any support."

Jacob jiggled from foot to foot and chewed on his bottom lip. "You need that in a time like this."

"Take a seat. You look like you could do with a strong cup of tea. Or maybe you'd like something to eat."

"I haven't eaten anything since yesterday. I keep thinking I need to eat but then remember that Adam will never get a chance to have a good meal or a glass of malt whiskey." He swiped a hand across his eyes.

"You shouldn't suffer because of that. Come on, I insist you sit down."

He stumbled to the kitchen table and sat. "Thanks. That's decent of you."

I brewed up a strong mug of tea and stirred sugar in it before handing it to him. "Drink that. How about I make you some Welsh rarebit and you can have some of my chocolate mocha cream cake? It's one of my favorite cakes to make."

"That sounds amazing." Jacob patted his stomach. "Now you're talking about food, I've realized how hungry I am."

"That's one thing I can definitely help with."

Five minutes later, I was sitting opposite Jacob as he tucked into two thick slices of toast with melted cheese, onion, and a dash of Worcestershire sauce on top.

"It must be hard losing an old friend," I said.

"It's the worst," Jacob said. "We weren't a big gang, but we just seemed to fit with each other. Adam was the party boy. He was a bit of a jock at school, loved rugby. And he was a popular guy, but he was always there when you needed him."

"Do the police know what happened?"

"They're working on it. Dad's got his security on it, too. They're the real experts. He's got three guys who look after the manor and his business interests. They're all ex-police, so I guess they'll figure things out if the local force is struggling."

"You make it sound like it wasn't an accident."

"Oh! I mean, it has to be. What else could have happened?" Jacob focused on his plate.

"Adam wasn't having any troubles that he talked to you about?"

He shrugged. "We weren't as close as we used to be. You know what it's like. People get older and grow apart. This was the first time I'd seen him in years. We kept in touch online, but that was about it. The party was an excuse to get the old gang back together and remember the good old days."

"I'm so sorry it ended like that. If your dad's team needs an extra hand, the castle security is great. You may have seen Campbell Milligan at the manor house? An extra set of eyes could speed things up."

"I don't know if we need it. I mean, from what I've heard so far, the police think it was an accident."

"What do you think happened? Is it unsafe on the veranda?"

Jacob glanced away before throwing down a crust. "Adam had a lot to drink last night, but he could handle his booze. He was always the one to ask for a last round, and he was always the last one standing."

"Well, I hope it gets figured out quickly. And the offer stands. I'm sure Campbell would be available if you needed the help."

"Let me run it past Dad, see what he thinks." He pushed his chair back.

"You don't have to leave. You haven't had any cake."

"I should get back. I've still got everyone staying at the manor house, and Dad's stressed by what's going on. I only popped over here to check in on you."

"Let me give you some cake to go." I quickly wrapped some chocolate mocha cream cake and handed it to him.

"Thanks. Sorry again about this mess. I'm sure it'll get sorted soon." He nodded a goodbye and left the kitchen.

I waited until I was certain Jacob was out of earshot before turning to the interior door. "I know you're listening, Campbell."

There was a shuffling, then the door inched open. Campbell appeared. "How did you know I was out here?"

"Because you're always sneaking around and listening into conversations," I said. "And you'd have spotted Jacob coming to the castle. You wouldn't have been able to resist seeing what he was here for."

He stepped through the door. "It's my job to be vigilant."

"Some may call that nosy."

He snorted a laugh. "I had to make sure you weren't hiding anything from me."

"Why would I do that? You're the one famous for hiding key information."

"Only because it's not relevant to you."

"It's always relevant."

"I'm not convinced. How does sticking your nose into my investigations help you make chocolate mocha cake?"

I arched an eyebrow and stared him down.

Campbell rolled his eyes. "Fine, so I was listening in. And I suppose I should say thank you."

I grinned at him. "I'm always happy to help. We both want in on this investigation. Jacob thinks it's a good idea to use your expertize. And we have Lady Philippa on our side. After I spoke to her this morning about what's been going on—"

"Holly! How many times do I have to tell you not to involve the family?"

"I can't help it if Lady Philippa orders me to her rooms to discuss murder. What am I supposed to do, sit in silence and refuse to answer her questions?"

"That's a great idea. Lady Philippa is a fragile, old woman. She's under strict instructions not to get excited by anything because it puts a strain on her heart."

"Don't let her catch you saying she's old and fragile, or she'll have your head. Anyway, we were talking about what happened to Adam—"

He lifted a hand. "If you're going to throw wild theories at me, at least make it worth my while. I'll have tea and cake."

"You make the tea. I'll fix up the cake."

With a dissatisfied grunt, he stalked to the cabinet and pulled out two mugs. "What does Lady Philippa think went on?"

"Let's say for a second, that you believe she has premonitions about people dying." I lifted a tray of chocolate mocha cream cake out of the chiller cabinet.

"Go on." He poured boiling water into the mugs.

"She saw Adam fall to his death. Just before he died, he was arguing with someone on the veranda. Maybe that argument led to a fight, and he was shoved over the edge."

"I suppose Lady Philippa didn't see the person Adam was arguing with before his fatal plummet." Campbell returned to the table and sat down with the tea.

"Sadly not. But she's convinced his death wasn't an accident."

"What about you? Do you buy into the murder theory?"

I brought over the cake and sat opposite him. "We need to keep an open mind."

"My mind is open," Campbell said. "I've been checking the backgrounds of everyone at the party."

"Did you find anyone with a motive to kill Adam?" I selected the largest piece of cake and bit into it.

"Nothing solid. Adam worked for a hedge fund in the city. He made himself a lot of money. His comments and posts on social media were all about his amazing lifestyle, vacations, and fast cars, that sort of thing."

"Any girlfriend? Could he have been having relationship trouble?"

"There are plenty of pictures of pretty women. None that seemed to stick."

"So he didn't like commitment. Maybe one of the women he was seeing didn't like that."

"And she snuck into a well-guarded manor house and killed him?" Campbell shook his head.

I toyed with the rest of my cake. "What about Bruce Jonas?"

Campbell nodded slowly. "He's at the top of my list. I'm looking hard at him."

"He wasn't with the rest of the group when Adam was pushed off the veranda."

"Possibly pushed off the veranda."

"Okay, *possibly* pushed. And when I talked to Bruce at the party, he seemed unsettled."

"Did he say anything about Adam that made you think he was up to something?"

"No, but he was worried and tense. Do you know much about him?"

"Probably no more than you. The guy has a limited online presence and a basic bank account. Nothing else."

"I heard he's been struggling."

"His mental health problems?"

I nodded. "I don't want to point the finger because he's not well, but someone needs to talk to him and see where he was at the time Adam died."

"I'll see what I can do."

"Bruce often spends time at the churchyard. You could try there."

Campbell stuffed cake in his mouth. "I'll do that."

"Keep me informed if you find out anything useful. After all, I'm getting you access to potential suspects."

"You're potentially getting me access to potential suspects. Things haven't been cleared yet. Lee could still block access to this investigation."

"They will be if Lady Philippa and Jacob have anything to do with it."

"Did Lady Philippa share anything else with you?"

"No." I stared into my tea before looking up at him. "I've been thinking about Eleanor Carrell's suicide."

His eyes narrowed. "You were asking about her last night."

"It's so strange. Teenage relationships break down all the time. She must have been very fragile to do something so devastating."

"Maybe she was. I don't know anything about the case."

"You should. After all, she used to date Adam."

"You're suggesting a ghost shoved Adam off the roof?"

"No! There's no such thing." Although my visits to Lady Philippa's rooms sometimes had me questioning that belief.

"Didn't you say Eleanor died ten years ago? I don't see how her death is relevant to what happened to Adam."

"I don't like loose ends."

"There are no loose ends. Eleanor had her heart broken and made a mistake. Ten years later, a guy she dated for five minutes died."

When Campbell put it like that, maybe I was thinking too far out of the box.

"I've got my eye on Bruce. Once I get a look around the site Adam fell from and talk to the partygoers, I'll have a clearer picture." Campbell licked his finger and pressed cake crumbs off his plate. "My money's on Bruce. This should be an easy case to solve if Adam was murdered."

I finished my cake. "You're probably right."

"I'm always right, Holmes. Now, parcel up some of that cake to go. I've got places to be."

"You've already had two slices."

"It's for the rest of my team."

"Sure it is." I wrapped up the remaining cake.

I could be overthinking this. Adam could simply have had too much to drink and fallen. Or he'd had a fight with Bruce, a man who was desperately unwell, and things got out of hand.

Whatever happened, the outcome was a sad one, and I wanted to make sure justice was done.

Chapter 8

I peered out the window at the front of my apartment into the gloom. "He's supposed to keep me informed. It's been hours. I've heard nothing." I looked at my cell phone. I'd sent three messages to Campbell. All had gone unanswered.

"You should know better than to trust a man." Gran had her feet up on my couch and a blanket over her knees. Saffron was fast asleep beside her. "Especially that one. He's so serious. He barely smiles."

"Campbell should tell me what's going on. I gave him a way into this investigation. He can't shut me out."

"Of course he can. He's a bull-headed alpha male. He'll do whatever he likes."

I sighed and turned away from the window. "I don't like being left out. I'm involved. I almost died!"

"Then be proactive. Go and get yourself involved. Be a thorn in Campbell's side until he has no choice but to include you."

"I usually am. But this case feels different. I can't put my finger on it. Everything seems muddled, like I'm looking through smoky glass and only seeing half of what I should."

"From what you've told me, it sounds straightforward enough. Adam either fell or was pushed by his sick friend. The tricky thing to figure out was if the push was accidental or deliberate."

"I wish I could get a look round and speak to everyone who was at the party. That would put my mind at rest. I'm frustrated because I can't get any information."

"Then what are you waiting for?" Gran shook her head. "Go get that information."

I pushed my hair off my face. "Campbell's supposed to be getting it. I should go after him and see what the problem is."

She pursed her lips. "You need to be careful chasing after a man. People will talk."

I paused from shrugging on my jacket. "Talk about what?"

"They may think you like him."

I tipped my head back and laughed. "I don't dislike Campbell, not anymore, but I don't like him the way you're implying. I have no plans to skip off into the sunset with Campbell on my arm. As you said, he's a stubborn alpha male. That gets frustrating to be around."

"He may be stubborn, but he's good-looking enough. I've seen him running in the morning. Those thighs could crack walnuts."

"Gran! You shouldn't be ogling the security," I said. "Besides, you have Ray. Isn't he your ideal man?"

"He's getting there. And he's been very sweet with helping me find a place to live. After I looked round that grotty studio apartment that had damp on the ceiling, I was at a loss where to turn. He's been asking around the village and several more places have shown up."

"That's great news. I'm happy things are going well for you two."

"He's different from the men I'm usually interested in. He's thoughtful and is always asking me questions about myself. I'm not used to it. It feels strange to be the center of a man's attention."

"You deserve someone nice, especially after what happened in your previous relationship." Gran hated to talk about the man who wooed her and stole her money, forcing her to turn to crime to make ends meet.

She stroked the blanket over her knees. "Change is good, but it takes some getting used to. I'm enjoying my time with Ray. We're not rushing anything."

"I need to go and probably not enjoy my time with Campbell. I have to know what's going on. I won't be long. I'll leave Meatball with you for company."

He was already snuggled up by her feet and seemed happy to stay there.

I marched over to the castle and spent half an hour walking around trying to find Campbell. There was no sign of him.

I took out my phone and sent another message. *Any update? Or did Lee kill you for treading on his toes?*

I headed to the kitchen. There were a couple of people on duty, and I nodded hello at them.

Whenever I needed to see Campbell, he was never around. Yet when I was up to no good, he was hovering like a buzzard chasing a field mouse.

I made up a box of chocolate mocha cream cake, grabbed a bike from the storage shed, and headed over to Marchwood Manor. If Campbell wasn't going to keep me informed, then Gran was right, I needed to do things for myself.

I didn't enjoy cycling in the dark, but it was barely dusk, and the bike had a great set of lights on the front and back. Plus, the lanes around Audley St. Mary were never busy, and local residents were usually considerate when they saw me out cycling.

I made the journey to Marchwood Manor in thirty minutes, secured the bike, and collected the box of cakes off the back. Hopefully, they'd give me a foot in the door, and I'd get to talk to Jacob and his friends.

"You just try it, and I'll break your face."

I froze. That was Campbell, and he sounded furious.

"I'm happy to toss you out of here. This is my territory. You don't get to come in and start asking questions." That sounded like Lee.

I crept closer, keeping my back to the wall of the manor house.

"Sir Richard okayed it. He wants this death resolved quickly. He's happy to use all resources—"

"I don't care what Sir Richard told you. He hasn't got a clue about the security needs of the manor house. That's what he pays me for. I don't need some failed squaddie messing things up."

I tensed as Campbell growled. I snuck closer and peered round the corner of the house. Campbell and Lee stood almost toe to toe, glowering at each other.

"You're in over your head. This death is bigger than you think," Lee said.

Campbell was silent for a second. "You're buying into the conspiracy idea?"

"Don't sound so surprised. If you knew Adam's background, it would make sense."

"Why don't you tell me?"

Lee smirked. "This is killing you, isn't it? I'm in charge here. I'm the one with the information. And I'll be the one who solves this case."

"You shouldn't hold grudges," Campbell said. "What happened is ancient history."

I tilted my head. What was he talking about?

"Yeah, and it cost me a promotion. And I had to leave the Army."

"You made bad decisions. That was your fault. I wasn't going to hide your dirty little secret," Campbell said.

"As you kept reminding me at the time, which is why you're getting no help from me. In fact, you're leaving right now. Don't come back."

"You can try to make me leave. Sir Richard gave me the okay to speak to everyone. He knows I can close cases."

"Sure you can. You probably got lucky the few times you did that." Lee shoved Campbell in the chest.

He backed up a couple of steps but remained standing. "You need to do the right thing by this family. If Adam's death wasn't an accident, you're in over your head."

"You don't give me enough credit. You never did." Lee pushed Campbell. "If I find you here again, you'll be walking away with a permanent limp."

"That sounds like a threat." Campbell shoved Lee back.

"No, old friend. It's a promise." Lee's hands flexed into fists.

I sucked in a breath, pulled back my shoulders, and strode around the side of the house. "There you are, Campbell. I've been looking for you."

Both men glared at each other for several seconds before Campbell stepped back. "What are you doing here, Holly?"

"I've come to see the family and make sure they're doing okay. Jacob was kind enough to check on me, so it only seemed right. Would either of you like cake? I've got chocolate mocha cream." I flipped open the lid and shoved the box between them. It just about slid past the puffed up chests and over-inflated muscles.

Lee swatted the box away. My delicious cakes sailed through the air and landed on the gravel.

"Hey! There was no need for that. I was being friendly. Everyone likes cake," I said.

"Not me. Sugar rots your teeth," Lee said, still glaring at Campbell.

"Apologize to Holly," Campbell said.

"Did I offend your girlfriend?" Lee bared his teeth. "I did her a favor. She could do with losing a few pounds."

Campbell growled at him. "Don't insult my friends."

"Friends with benefits, I reckon," Lee said.

"That's enough." I squeezed in between them and placed a hand on each solidly muscled chest. "What will this look like to your employer, Lee? You start a brawl with Campbell and you could lose your job."

"He doesn't deserve a job here," Campbell said. "The guy's a joke."

"Right now, you'll both look like jokes if this goes any further. I suggest you both walk away while you still can."

"He wouldn't be able to hurt me if I had one arm tied behind my back," Lee said. "Campbell's past his prime."

"You never had a prime," Campbell said.

"I'm sure you are both magnificent, but now isn't the time to prove it. We're all here for the same thing. We want to make sure Adam gets justice for what happened to him."

"Why do you care?" Lee said.

I looked at them both. Neither seemed primed to tear the other's head off, but I'd keep a close watch just in case. "I care because a man is dead."

"And?" Lee said. "You didn't know the guy. Aren't you some servant over at the castle?"

"I'm the best baker they have in the kitchen," I said. "You'd have known that if you'd tried my chocolate mocha cake rather than tossing it in the dirt."

He lifted one shoulder. "I'm so impressed. So, you make a few cakes for the Audley family. I still don't see why you have to be involved in this case."

"Holly can have useful ideas about these things," Campbell said. "She's insightful."

Lee's jaw dropped. "You're kidding me. She's your secret weapon? She's the reason you've been solving these mysteries at the castle?"

Campbell's color rose. "I wouldn't go that far. She has a way to get people to talk, though. She disarms them."

He was full of compliments this evening.

Lee tipped back his head and roared out a laugh. "I don't believe it. You've got a woman fighting your battles. You've really lost your edge, old man."

"Keep your mouth shut," Campbell said. "You have no idea what you're talking about."

"Oh, I do. When I heard you'd taken the role at Audley Castle, I wondered what had happened to you. You've gone soft. There was a time when you wouldn't let anyone get in your way. And here you are, being dictated to by Little Miss Chubby Baker."

I jabbed Lee in the chest with a finger. "I've already told you, it's water weight. And I wish I could dictate to Campbell, but he's as stubborn as a mule. I can't get him to do anything. Believe me, he's not soft."

Lee smirked. "What exactly do you want him to do to you?"

"That's enough," Campbell said, rage tearing through his words and making them grunt out of him.

"Yeah, I reckon it is. Get out of here, before I call in my team and have you both evicted." Lee turned and strode away.

Campbell turned on me, and I shrank at the fury blazing in his eyes. "What are you doing here?"

"Chasing after you, since you won't return my messages. You said you'd keep me informed about the investigation."

"So when you didn't hear from me, you took things into your own hands? You snuck over here with your cakes and tried to snoop."

"As you said, I have a way of disarming people." I stared forlornly at the lost cakes. Lee must have a heart of stone to destroy something so delicious.

"I was going to keep you informed, but I was dealing with that jerk. He distracted me," Campbell said.

"You could have sent me a single message, even if it was just to say you'd drop by when you were done here. I was thinking the worst."

"You thought something bad happened to me?"

"No! I figured out a long time ago that you're invincible. I thought you might have changed your mind. You were shutting me out as usual."

He glowered at me. "Maybe I should. I don't want you stalking me when I don't return a message after five minutes. That makes you more like a possessive girlfriend than a partner."

"You want me to be your official sleuthing partner?" I grinned up at him.

He let out a long sigh and tilted his head back so he was staring at the darkening sky. "Holly, there's no point in me reporting back to you all the time, not until I have all the information."

"We are still working together, though?"

He looked down at me. "I'm going to regret this, but we are."

"That's something. So, did Lee give you any useful information?"

His eyes narrowed. "How long were you listening into our conversation?"

"Long enough to know you have a real problem with each other. What happened between you two?"

"I've already said, long story. It's not relevant now."

"It is if you're going to work with him."

"I'll never work with that loser again. All you need to know is he holds a grudge against me. I pulled him up when he let his standards slip, and he hated that. Now, he's a barrier between getting access to what I need."

"What *we* need."

"It's the same thing."

"Surely, if Sir Richard said it's okay for you to be involved, Lee can't have a problem."

"In theory, but Sir Richard isn't always around. Lee's going to cause trouble."

"Then we cause trouble right back. Perhaps the next time I come with offerings of cake, I'll mix a little something extra into it."

"You're thinking about poisoning Lee?"

"No! But maybe some prune juice or some kind of natural laxative. Get him chained to the toilet for a couple of hours. It'll give us time to poke around."

"Good luck with that. Lee follows a rigid diet to keep in shape. All high protein and limited carbs. You won't find him snacking on cupcakes."

"You don't follow a rigid diet, and it doesn't do you any harm." I poked him in the stomach. My finger bent back as I met a wall of muscle.

"I work out hard to ensure I can indulge in your cakes. Anyway, less talk about incapacitating Lee. I have a mystery to solve."

"*We* have a mystery to solve."

"Holmes, you'd try the patience of a saint."

"Not if I gave him chocolate mocha cream cake to cheer him up. Okay, I have a question. Why are you both focusing on the alien conspiracy theory? I heard you talking about it with Lee."

"He's more focused on that idea than I am. He won't give me the details, but he's got some information. And

I've been looking into it, too."

"Come off it. You can't believe there's a government cover-up about secret alien bases across the world. It's too weird."

"It may seem weird to you, but the world doesn't always operate the way it should. I've seen things and even done a few things that led me to believe there are greater forces at work."

I scoffed out a laugh. He had to be teasing me. My laughter died when he didn't crack a smile. "You really think this is about some conspiracy cover-up? You figured it was a straight forward accident yesterday. Not even a murder."

He looked over my head into the distance.

"Campbell, we're working together. I need to know everything."

"Sometimes you don't. You should stay out of this. And before you argue with me, I'm not saying that because you're getting in my way. I'm saying it for your own safety."

My stomach did a funny flip-flop. The vague sense of unease I'd carried with me since Adam died, intensified. "Do you think a little green man is coming to take me away?"

He didn't laugh. He didn't even breathe.

"That was a joke," I said.

"Hilarious."

"Conspiracy theories are just that. There's never proof to back them up. Or is there? What have you found out?" I was joking again, sort of.

He cracked his jaw. "The group staying at Marchwood Manor poked their noses into something they shouldn't."

"What did they discover?"

"I'm not sure. It was years ago. Lee knows something, but he's not sharing. He kept saying it was classified. I've got higher military clearance than him, so I know that's garbage. But he wouldn't give up his source. I'll keep looking into it."

"It's something about aliens? Should we get our laser guns out, just in case?"

"Why the fixation on aliens?"

"Blame Princess Alice. She got me thinking about them. If it's not little green men, is it some government cover-up?"

"It's possible."

I snorted a laugh. "I'm not buying that."

"What are you struggling with?"

"All of it."

"Holly, please, for once, do as I ask. Stay out of this."

I shook my head. "I'm involved. I was there when Adam died."

"Which was unfortunate. Walk away now, while you can."

"While I can?" The sternness in his gaze unsettled me. "You make it sound as if my life is at risk."

"Hopefully, it's not."

"Do I need to start sleeping with a kitchen knife under my pillow?"

"I'm sure everything will be fine. I need to do more digging, and I need to get the information out of Lee."

"Let's start with an easy question. The thing we're certain about. We all think it was murder?"

"Yes. I'm leaning toward that."

"Now for a trickier question if we're running with the conspiracy theory. Could it have something to do with the food lab?"

"Food lab? What are you talking about?"

"It's something Dexter mentioned. He said the group went to this lab and looked around. I found pictures of it online. It was all high fences and barbed wire. There were also guards with guns. Lady Philippa thought it was a food testing laboratory."

"Where exactly are you talking about?"

"Appledore."

He scrubbed his chin. "The site over by the reservoir?"

"Yes, that's the place. Do you know anything about it?"

His eyebrows pinched together. "It wasn't a food testing lab."

"What was it?"

He huffed out a breath. "A government testing site."

"If you tell me they were running tests on aliens, I'm going to need a vacation."

"You really want to know?"

"Of course!"

"Viral weapons."

"Viral what? Why would they do such a thing in Appledore?"

"Because of the location. There are dozens of places like that one all over the country. The government would set up discreet units in small places with a low population. It meant fewer people poked their nose in to find out what was going on. They'd pick spots in forests or hilly locations that discouraged people from dropping in to make friends with their new neighbors."

"But ... viral weapons. That's dangerous. What if there was an accident or an explosion? The area could have been infected with whatever viruses they were testing."

"Again, I'll point you back to why they chose areas where not many people lived."

"Maybe Jacob and his friends visited this testing site and found something they shouldn't."

"Which is even more reason for you to stay out of this. If Adam's death links back to the government or any other agency, this could be dangerous."

"I don't believe it. I don't see any proof that this is anything more than a simple murder. A fight gone wrong, or an old score settled."

"And you won't find any proof, so long as you stop looking."

"There's still a murder to solve. Someone killed Adam."

"Maybe that someone has power and influence. Are you really sure you want in on this?"

The concern in Campbell's voice made me pause. My gut had been cramping ever since this mystery started. I should listen to it and back away while I could. But conspiracy theories, alien or not? No way.

"Holly, make the right choice," Campbell said. "Stay out of this mystery. It's for your own good."

Chapter 9

I blinked my gritty-feeling eyes as I poured a strong mug of coffee the next morning. I'd probably only gotten two hours' sleep last night after my encounter with Lee and Campbell at Marchwood Manor.

In the cold light of day, I couldn't believe Campbell about the viral weapons testing. I needed to do my own research. He must have made a mistake. Even if there was such a place located in Appledore, how was it linked to Adam's death? It couldn't be, could it?

"Good morning." Gran strolled into the kitchen, dressed in a pale pink linen suit, her hair neatly styled and a full face of make-up on. "I didn't hear you come in last night."

"I was late back." After speaking to Campbell, I'd cycled around for a while in the castle grounds, trying to get my thoughts in order. It hadn't helped.

"Did you have any luck with Campbell?" She accepted a mug of coffee from me as she sat at the table.

Saffron bounced around with Meatball. They were both hopeful of getting breakfast treats off the table.

"Sort of. He was at Marchwood Manor."

"That's my girl. Being proactive and getting to the bottom of things."

I joined her at the table. "That's just it. I'm worried I've gotten myself in the middle of something I don't know how to handle."

"You found out it was murder?"

My mouth twisted to the side. "Gran, what do you think about conspiracy theories?"

"I think most of them are made up by teenage boys with too much time on their hands and free access to dubious sources of information online. Why do you ask?"

"There's this idea going around that Adam's death was linked to some government cover-up."

She regarded me in silence for several seconds. "You can't believe that."

"I don't, not really, but Campbell seemed convinced last night. And the Marchwood Manor security are looking at that angle. Apparently, they've got information that they refuse to share. It's directing them to this cover-up idea."

"More likely, they're trying to make this into something big, so everyone will be impressed when they solve it. From what I've heard about this Lee character, he's not a nice man."

"I can confirm that. He threw my chocolate mocha cream cake on the ground last night."

"He's making this conspiracy nonsense up to look impressive. Some men do that. They have to because it makes up for certain physical failings."

"I don't want to think about Lee's physical failings. But the evidence has to be credible. He couldn't make it up, or he'd get found out. Campbell's also looking into this and so are the local police."

"Lay out the facts before we take a stroll along Conspiracy Avenue," Gran said. "What do you know? That'll help to see if this is some scary cover-up or simply a tragic mistake."

"The only fact I should focus on is that Adam is dead. Until the police or Marchwood Manor security figure out what happened to him, I shouldn't make connections where there aren't any."

"There you go. You've solved the problem. Focus on what happened to that young man. Perhaps this was an awful accident."

"I hope so. An accident is much more plausible than murder by a little green man."

"And now aliens are involved!" She shook her head. "No, this was done by a human hand, accident or not."

"Thanks. I needed to talk to someone with a level head."

"I wouldn't say I'm always level, but I know nonsense when I hear it."

I ran my gaze over Gran's outfit. "You look nice."

"I have another date with Ray. Well, I say a date. We're going for breakfast, then we're taking a look round some places he found me that are available to rent."

"That'll be fun. But you don't have to rush anything. You can stay here as long as you like. It's been nice having the company. And now Meatball and Saffron are getting along better, there's no reason to leave."

"And it's been wonderful staying with you, but I can't live here forever. I'm an independent woman. I need to make my own way in the world, especially now I have so much freedom."

"Well, I hope one of these places is right for you."

"If they aren't, I'll keep looking until I find the right one." She patted my arm. "You stay safe today if you're going to keep poking around in this murder. I should teach you the self-defence moves I learned while inside."

My eyes widened. "What kind of moves are we talking about?"

"A hard jab to someone's eyeballs always does the trick," Gran said. "If they can't see, they can't fight you."

"You fought someone in prison?"

She tapped the side of her nose. "It's best you don't know all my secrets." There was a knock at the front door. Gran hurried over to open it. "That must be Ray."

When she pulled the door open, Alice and Rupert stood outside.

"Hello! We're here to see if Holly can come out to play," Alice said.

I chuckled as I stood from my seat. "Come in, you two. What are you doing up so early?"

Alice bustled into the kitchen, followed by a sleepy looking Rupert. "We're here to take you out. I know you don't start work for an hour and a half, so you've got time."

"Where do you want to go?" I said.

Rupert yawned loudly. "Sorry about this. I told Alice it was too early, but she dragged me out of bed, anyway. She wants us to go cold water swimming in our mermaid tails."

"What's this?" Gran strolled over. "You have mermaid tails?"

"Holly introduced us to the wonderful world of mermaid swimming," Alice said. "She took as for these amazing lessons. As a reward for finding me a brilliant new hobby, I got us custom made mermaid tails. They're waiting for us by the lake."

I glanced out the window. Although the sun was shining, the water would still be freezing. "Are you sure it's safe?"

"Are you worried a giant pike might nibble on your toes?" Alice said.

"There are pike in there?" I said.

Rupert shook his head. "No, it's safe. There may be a few ducks waddling around, but there's nothing in the lake that's a threat."

"And it'll do you good. Take your mind off that horrible business at Marchwood Manor," Alice said. "Although I do expect an update. You haven't been keeping me in the loop, and Campbell has barely been around, so I haven't been able to grill him. And remember, Granny tipped you off about the murder, so don't leave us out."

Gran tilted her head. "Does Lady Philippa have a background in criminology?"

"No, nothing like that," I said.

"Yet she knows about murder? I can't imagine a lady working for the police. Oh, no, let me guess. Was she a spy? Did she go undercover to gather enemy secrets?" Gran said.

"No. At least, I don't think Lady Philippa was a spy." I looked at Alice.

She giggled. "Granny has never been a spy. She has a … special gift."

"A gift? What are we talking about?" Gran said.

"Let's talk about Lady Philippa's gift another time," I said. "For now, it looks like Adam's death wasn't an accident. Although I'm not sure what I can do to help."

"A dunk in the cold water will clarify your thoughts," Alice said. "Come on, no stalling because it's chilly. We've got our mermaid tails to enjoy. Go get changed into something you can swim in."

I dashed to my room, grabbed my costume, had a quick freshen up in the bathroom, and changed.

I waved goodbye to Gran and headed along the path with Rupert, Alice, and Meatball.

"I had several more private lessons with the amazing mermaid tutor from the public pool," Alice said. "She has mermaid blood running through her veins."

"You didn't need them," Rupert said. "You're already a natural mermaid."

"It's a shame you aren't a natural merman," Alice said. "Didn't you almost drown the first time we tried out our tails?"

"Holly saved me," he said. "She always comes to my rescue when I need her."

I grinned and blushed. "You'd do the same for me. So, where are our tails?"

"Next to that big old willow by the edge of the lake," Alice said. "We can change and dive right in."

I discovered my beautiful shimmering pink and blue mermaid tail laid out for me. I stroked my fingers along the soft waterproof material.

"Aren't they divine?" Alice picked hers up. "We can change here. Rupert's got his tail, so he'll be too busy squeezing into it to peek at you."

I ducked behind the tree, shimmied off my jeans and top, and headed to the water's edge with my tail over one arm.

I dipped a toe in and yanked it out. "Alice! This is icy."

"It's fine. I've been reading about the benefits of swimming in cold water," she said. "It improves circulation, lowers blood pressure, burns fat, boosts your metabolism, and it's fun."

"Since when was being freezing cold fun?"

"Don't be such a grump. You're usually up for a new fitness challenge." Alice strode over, slid into her mermaid tail, and sat on the muddy bank. She swung her legs and dipped the end of her tail in the water. "Oh! It is a little on the chilly side. Rupert, contact the castle and have them bring out our wetsuits."

"Wetsuits! We aren't scuba diving," he said from behind the willow tree.

"No, but we need extra layers to keep out the chill."

"I don't suppose you've got a spare one for me?" I said.

"Of course. We have spares of everything," Alice said. "Rupert! Make sure they grab one for Holly, too."

Rupert grumbled under his breath as he made the call. "They'll be ten minutes."

"That gives you time to tell me what's been going on in Adam's murder investigation." Alice flipped her tail, showering me with icy droplets of water. "What have you discovered?"

"That I should stay out of it. It seems a bit ... messy."

"You can never resist a murder," she said. "What's got you so concerned about this one?"

"It's something Campbell said yesterday. He confronted the head of security at Marchwood Manor, Lee Mahoney."

"I can't stand that man. Lee, not Campbell. He pretends to be polite and well-mannered, but I've seen him when he thought my attention was diverted. He rolls his eyes and tuts, makes out that we're an inconvenience for him. I don't like him one little bit. Is he causing problems?"

"He is being stubborn. But it's more than that. He's got information that Adam's death has to do with a conspiracy theory."

Alice clapped her hands. "My alien theory is true. I told you they were real."

"Aliens weren't really discussed as the reason behind the death."

"They never are. That's how they've managed to stay hidden for so long."

"Campbell is making the investigation sound very mission impossible. Government secrets, cover-ups, mystery. He has me worried."

"That should be right up your street," Alice said.

"I don't want to go head-to-head with a scary government agency!"

"Holly, you can't leave this alone. This needs your input. If aliens are involved, they'll need someone to take care of them."

"I have no plans to foster any aliens. And I don't have the skills to go up against a secret power. Although I can't believe this has anything to do with some big cover-up. I don't mind asking a few questions and bribing people with cake when I need information, but this is too complicated."

"You had it figured out when we had breakfast with Granny," Alice said. "You said that Bruce Jonas has no alibi. Have you questioned him?"

"No, but if I was heading up this investigation, I'd be focused on him. Campbell was, initially. He's done background checks on everyone at the party."

"I tell you what, we'll deal with this." Alice jabbed a finger at Rupert as he emerged from behind the tree.

"What are you planning on doing?" I said.

"I often see Bruce when I'm passing the churchyard. And although he can be intense when I talk to him, he's always polite. We'll go and speak to him, won't we, Rupert?"

"Are you sure that's a good idea? After all, he is a suspect in a murder investigation," Rupert said.

"Maybe you should leave this to the police and Campbell," I said. "Rupert's right. If Bruce is unstable, he could react badly to being questioned about Adam."

"It's either pursue that line of inquiry or believe in my aliens," Alice said.

"What's this about aliens?" Rupert said.

"It's nothing. There's no such thing as aliens," I said. "Definitely not around Audley St. Mary."

"There are so." Alice shuffled closer to the water. "Besides, I like Bruce. I'm not afraid of him. He's always grateful when I make Campbell give him a sandwich or buy him a coffee when I spot him in the village. He won't do me any harm. We can go after we've had our swim."

"I could come with you, but it'll have to be after work this evening," I said.

"No, it's no bother. I was going to the dress shop in the village today, anyway. We can make a short stop at the churchyard and have a chat with Bruce, get this cleared up."

"Question him gently," I said. "Just see if he has an alibi for the time Adam died. Bruce has had a rough time. He's on strong medication and it gives him hallucinations. Keep him calm and the conversation light."

"We'll be careful. Besides, I can run faster than Rupert. If there's any trouble, all I need to do is outrun my lazy brother," Alice said.

"You're not funny," Rupert muttered.

"Oh look, here come our wetsuits. Rupert, go collect them. I can barely move in my tail." Alice pointed at the approaching SUV rumbling over the grass.

Rupert grumbled again before hurrying over to the car and collecting the three wetsuits.

After a brief struggle, I was in my wetsuit, and Rupert was wearing his merman tail.

"Is everyone ready?" Alice's blue eyes sparkled as she looked at us. "It's time to be mermaids."

I glanced at Rupert and bit my lip. He looked equally worried.

Alice didn't hesitate. She wiggled herself into the water and swam away. She flipped onto her back. "What are you both waiting for? Get in."

Meatball barked. He bounced on his paws by the edge of the lake.

"Go on," I said to him. "In you go if you want to."

"Woof!" He launched into the lake, showering me with spray, then doggy paddled after Alice, his little tail in the air.

"I wish I could show as much enthusiasm about diving in," Rupert said.

"Me, too."

"We could always make a run for it," Rupert said. "Well, a slow waddle in our tails. I can order us a piping hot breakfast, and we can forget this horrible event ever happened."

"As tempting as that is, Alice will never forgive me if I don't try cold water swimming in my mermaid tail. Let's give it a go. On three?"

He grimaced, but then nodded. "On three."

"One, two, three!" I slid into the water, gasping as the icy liquid engulfed me. But the tail and wetsuit did a great job of keeping out the worst of the cold.

I swam frantically for several minutes, trying to warm up. Soon my skin was tingling, and I felt like I was glowing from the inside.

"Isn't this great?" Alice was way ahead of us as she flipped and twirled in her mermaid tail.

Meatball kept chasing her around the lake, barking with joy and splashing everyone he passed.

After doing a couple of circuits of the lake, my head felt clearer. And that clear head led me to a decision. I should stay out of this murder investigation. Even if this was a simple murder and Bruce killed Adam, I didn't want to get in the middle of two head-butting alpha males. Campbell and Lee were welcome to this mystery.

Half an hour of glorious cold water swimming later and I was back on the bank, drying myself with a large fluffy towel Alice provided for me.

"Did you enjoy it?" she said. "We could do this every morning. It's so much better than running. And your cheeks have a lovely glow. You look five years younger."

I shivered as I rubbed my damp hair. "I did enjoy it. I wasn't sure I would, but once I got moving, the numbness went away."

"And the health benefits go on for hours after your swim," Alice said.

"I'm more of a fair weather swimmer," Rupert said. His hair was plastered across his forehead and he had a glum look on his face. "I can't feel my toes. You don't think there's been any permanent damage to them?"

"Don't be such a wimp." Alice threw a wet towel at him. "You were swimming too slowly, that's why you can't feel anything. And you kept staring at Holly, which didn't help. You can't swim straight if you're leering at her."

"I wasn't leering," he said. "Well, I was looking now and again to check she was doing okay. There's nothing wrong with that."

"Of course not. Thanks, Rupert." I quickly dried Meatball, then bundled up the towel, not keen on getting in the middle of a brother and sister argument. "I need to get going. I can't be late for work."

"Leave the tail and wet things with us," Alice said. "I'll have your tail dried and clean for the next time."

I set my tail down, gave them a wave, and headed off to the apartment with Meatball to grab my things and get ready for work.

I rounded the corner, and a flash of movement caught my attention. I'd only caught a glimpse, but there'd been a man in a black suit standing by a bush. He stepped back the second I appeared.

"What do you think he wants, Meatball?" I glanced at my apartment, which was a short walk away, then back to the bush. There was no sign of the man coming back.

It was usual to see the gardening team out at this time of the morning, but no one else. And the man wasn't in work overalls, so I didn't think he was employed around here.

I hurried over to the bush and peered round it. There was no one there. I looked round. Whoever it was, they'd vanished.

I glanced down at Meatball.

He wagged his tail at me, not seeming concerned. He was probably thinking about breakfast.

"Maybe he's a friend of the family who got lost." I looked back at the castle. "I don't think Alice or Rupert have anyone staying with them."

"Woof, woof!"

"No, it'll have to remain a mystery. I'll ask them about him later. Come on, we both need some breakfast, then I have to get to work."

Chapter 10

I yawned as I pulled off my apron, hung it up, and then headed out the back door of the kitchen. We'd had another busy day, and I'd felt every minute of it thanks to my poor night of sleep.

I collected Meatball from his kennel, and we headed toward the wood for his evening walk.

"What would you like for dinner, tonight? You've got duck kibble, game-flavored kibble, and beef kibble. Or I spotted some cottage pie left out for the staff that didn't sell in the café. It looked delicious. I could treat you to a little of that. Gran would like it, too."

"Woof, woof, woof!" He danced in front of me, always excited by our conversations about food. Well, I got excited talking about food, and Meatball fed off my energy.

"We'll have to find out how Gran got on with her apartment search today," I said. "It's a shame she has to go. I reckon you'll miss Saffron."

Meatball slowed, and his eyes narrowed a fraction. He was usually a good boy, but he'd been a bit jealous of Saffron. He loved to be the center of attention.

"You've been great, putting up with her tantrums when she doesn't get her own way. And, I'll be honest, I won't miss sharing a bathroom with someone. Did you notice, Gran squeezes the toothpaste from the middle?"

Meatball barked. His ears pricked, and he raced in front of me, through the trees and deeper into the wood.

"No bothering the squirrels! They never do anything mean to you."

The sound of a dry branch breaking had me turning. I looked around. "Is anybody there?"

There was silence in response.

I increased my pace. "Meatball, come here, boy."

There was no sign of him.

A scraping, cracking sound made me jump. My hand flew to my chest as I peered through the trees. Someone was watching me.

My heart was in my throat as I stared at them. "Who's there? I can see you. Come out."

There was silence for a second, then Bruce Jonas appeared through the trees.

"Bruce! What are you doing out here?" I glanced around, suddenly aware of how isolated I was.

"Are you alone?" He had leaves sticking out of his hair, his face was pale, and he was sweating.

"Other than my dog, Meatball, yes. What's the matter? Are you okay?"

He scraped a dirty hand down his face. "I had to hide. They're after me."

"Who's after you?" My hand went to my pocket. I was reassured by the feel of my cell phone. If anything went wrong, I could make a run for it and call the police for help.

"They came looking around my home. I had to leave. It's no longer safe there."

"Your home being the churchyard?"

He nodded. "They know where I live now. I can't go back there. It's been compromised. They'll have someone posted, lurking in the shadows, waiting for me to return."

The poor guy was in a mess. "Bruce, there's no one after you."

"There has been for years. I get no peace. They're always listening in or watching me. I have to be so careful." His gaze flashed around the woods, and every muscle appeared tense, as if he was about to flee.

"Why don't you come back with me? Maybe talking about it will help. I was planning on having cottage pie for dinner if you'd like some."

"I can't put you at risk. I didn't want anybody to know I was in the woods, but then you came along with your dog and he sniffed me out. I've always kept a low profile. And after what happened to Adam, it showed I was right to do so. Everyone thinks I'm crazy, but I know the truth."

"The truth about what?"

He pressed a finger to his lips. "It's a secret."

"I'm sorry about what happened to Adam. It must have been such a shock."

"It was, but it wasn't a surprise. They were bound to catch up with us, eventually."

"You know someone who had a problem with Adam?"

He nodded and licked his cracked lips.

"You don't think his death was an accident?"

"Of course it wasn't. Adam was murdered." Bruce jumped and spun around. "Did you hear that?"

"It's just the wind in the trees. I don't think anyone else is out here. I'm one of the few people who use this area of the woods because it's a good place to bring Meatball."

Bruce looked around for several seconds before turning back to me. "There are bad people coming for us. I can't stop them. It's gone too far."

I shook my head. Poor Bruce. This was his illness talking. "Who are these people?"

He lifted the camera around his neck and shot several pictures. "I don't know their names. They live in the shadows. Shadow people. Evil people."

"You seem really scared. Let me help you."

"You can't help. Nobody can. They're here to tidy up the loose ends, and I'm one of them."

"One of these people wants to hurt you?"

He scratched his fingers through his beard. "They do. You see, I love to record things. Take real pictures and videos, not just to put online. That's not the same thing."

"I don't think I've ever seen you without your camera."

"I sleep with it. And I have years of film footage. You never know when bad things will happen. If you have no record of them, then there's no proof."

"Is that why someone's after you? You took a picture of them doing something they shouldn't?"

He closed his eyes and nodded.

My heart thundered in my chest. Had he got something on Adam? He confronted him about it, and they fought? "What did you record?"

"Something I'm going to be killed for. They want me dead." When he opened his eyes, the desperation in them made my throat tighten. "I should never have come to the party. I tried to talk Jacob out of hosting it, but he said it would be fun. We were older and wiser, and no one cared about the past. It was time to move on."

"Move on from what?"

"I should go." Bruce took several steps in one direction, then pivoted and paced the other way. "I've already said too much."

"Bruce, wait! You were at the party when Adam died."

"When he was murdered."

"Yes, possibly, when he was murdered. Did you see anything? Was there anyone around acting suspiciously? His death is being looked into, but there aren't many clues to go on."

"Of course there won't be evidence. They're clever. They've covered it up. Just like they do with everything. You can't trust anybody."

"Where were you when Adam died?"

Bruce froze to the spot. His back was to me, and his shoulders hunched. "I was with Jacob."

"You were? I didn't see you."

"Because you weren't paying attention. People never do." He spun round to face me. "I was there. Jacob will back me up. We look out for each other."

"You weren't on the veranda with Adam?"

"Why would I have been up there? You can't blame this on me." Bruce let out a gasp and scrubbed at his eyes.

"I'm not. I just want to get to the truth. Perhaps you could let me see the footage of the party you recorded. There might be clues on there. You might have some film or a picture of someone who shouldn't have been at the party. Maybe that person killed Adam."

"No! You can't see that. This has nothing to do with you. Stay away from me. Stay out of this. If you keep poking around, you'll end up dead, too."

"Bruce, I want to help you. Perhaps if you talk to the police, tell them what you saw that night, we could figure out what happened to Adam."

"You can't make me do anything." He lunged and shoved me.

I lost my balance and fell to the ground. By the time I'd flipped over, Bruce had vanished.

I rubbed my elbow where I'd bashed it and scrambled to my feet. I looked around but had no idea which direction Bruce had run. He'd gone.

"Oh, Bruce, what did you do?" He hadn't been outside Marchwood Manor with Jacob and the others. I'd have seen him. He'd just lied to me about his alibi. Why would he do that if he didn't have something to hide?

I brushed dirt off my clothing and rubbed my sore elbow. "Meatball, come on. We need to get moving."

There were several barks in reply, but he didn't make an appearance.

I headed toward the barking. I'd have to tell Campbell about my encounter with Bruce. It wouldn't look good for him, but he seemed guilty. He was jumpy, anxious, and paranoid. I couldn't believe what he was saying about someone watching him and wanting him dead. Bruce was a sick man, and he desperately needed help. I hoped I'd be able to get that for him.

A movement caught my eye, and I peered through the trees. "Bruce, is that you? I didn't mean to frighten you. I was trying to help." I hurried in the direction of the movement.

I lost sight of Bruce for a minute but then saw a flash of black and slowed. My heart did the opposite as it jackhammered in my chest.

Bruce hadn't been wearing anything black. He'd worn a thick brown hoodie and a grubby pair of dark jeans.

"Hey! Wait up. Are you lost?" I raced after the person, scrambling over fallen branches in my haste to reach them. I couldn't be certain, but maybe this was the man in black who'd been watching me this morning.

"You're not getting away this time," I muttered as I dashed through the trees.

I stepped onto a small overgrown path and looked around.

There was silence. No birds singing, no shuffling sounds of small forest animals. Where had he gone? And why was he watching me?

I glanced over my shoulder as a shiver of unease ran down my spine. I couldn't believe this big conspiracy theory, but why was there suddenly a strange man in black lurking around the castle keeping an eye on things?

Whoever it was, there was no sign of him now. "Meatball, we really need to leave."

He barked, acknowledging me, but I could tell by the excited tone that he'd found something he was interested in and had no plans to leave any time soon.

"You'd better not be snuffling around some dead animal. And if you've rolled in fox poop, we're heading straight for the bath when we get home." I headed back into the trees.

I'd only gone a dozen steps, when an arm clamped around my middle from behind me and a hand covered my mouth.

I tried to scream, but it came out as a muffled gurgle as I was pressed against a solid chest.

"You need to stop poking around in things that don't concern you." The voice was low, growly, and male.

I struggled in his grip, but he kept a tight hold of me, and I could barely move. I kicked back with a foot but didn't make contact.

"You're playing a dangerous game. Leave the past where it is," he said.

The past? What was he talking about?

"And tell your friends and loved ones to do the same if they value their lives."

I'd had enough. No one threatened my friends. I fisted my hands and drove my elbow back into the man's stomach.

His breath shot out, but he remained clamped around me. "Keep interfering and you'll face the consequences." He released me so suddenly that I stumbled and almost fell.

Harsh barking filled my ears. Meatball! I couldn't let this mystery man hurt my best furry buddy.

I was turning to confront the man, when a bone-jarring thud connected on my left temple, and everything went black.

Chapter 11

The smell of dirt and dried leaves drifted up my nose as my eyes inched open. The left side of my head throbbed, and my stomach churned.

I was about to move, but froze. What if my attacker was still here? He could be waiting to see if I was dead.

A warm, damp nose nudged my ear. Meatball whined softly and licked my cheek.

"Oh! You're okay." I scrambled up onto my knees and grabbed him for a cuddle before checking him over. "You're such a brave boy. You must have scared the man away with all that barking. I was worried he may have hurt you."

He licked my cheek again and snuffled around the tender spot on my head.

A quick look around showed me I'd been unconscious for hours. It was almost dark, and I was freezing cold.

I kept hold of Meatball as I climbed to my feet, my knees wobbly. "Let's get out of here."

I hurried through the trees, keeping a watchful eye out for anyone coming after us, my paranoid radar on overdrive.

What had that man wanted? Why was he warning us off? Perhaps Campbell was right, and something big was going on here. Maybe a government cover-up, after all.

My hand shook so badly I could barely get the key in the lock once I was back at my apartment.

I stumbled through the door, keeping Meatball clutched to my chest. "Gran, are you home?"

There was only a small sidelight on, and the silence in the apartment told me there was no one there.

I gulped. Or was there? I set Meatball down and made short work of locking the door behind me and checking all the windows. I also looked in every closet and under the bed, just to be on the safe side.

"All clear, Meatball." I peered into the gloom outside the apartment before pulling the curtains.

Meatball stayed glued to my heels, whining softly now and again and nudging me.

I petted his head. "We're fine. We've just had a shock, that's all. We need something to help with that." I headed to the kitchen and dug out his favorite kind of meaty chew strip from the cupboard and fed him one.

As he ate it, I ran my hands over him again to double check he was fine. Other than a bit of mud in his fur, he was perfect.

I, however, didn't feel so great. My head ached like an elephant had kicked me. I may have a concussion. That guy didn't hit me softly. Maybe he'd intended to kill me. Could he be the one behind Adam's death?

"This calls for my special hot chocolate." I pulled out a tub of cocoa, marshmallows, and whipped cream from the fridge. I heated milk and mixed myself a rich, delicious sugary drink. It was exactly what I needed to take the edge off the shock.

I sat at the table, my hands still shaking as I took a sip. It was only then that I spotted the note.

Gone out with Ray. Don't wait up! Gran xx.

Since Gran wasn't here to talk to, I needed to do some figuring out on my own. I opened my laptop and ran a search for a virus testing facility in Appledore. I hadn't believed Campbell, but this incident had me wondering just what was going on.

Nothing was listed, other than a few blog posts on strange conspiracy websites that talked about deadly weapons, tests on innocent populations, and lizards who were running the government. Surely, if such a place existed, there'd have to be registration documents. It wouldn't be easy to start testing viral weapons without the appropriate licenses.

"Maybe it would if it was supposed to be kept a secret," I muttered. "Campbell said these bases were set up in out of the way locations so people wouldn't talk about them. Maybe they don't publish the licenses to keep the public away and avoid panic."

Meatball rested his nose against my leg and woofed softly.

"Do you think something strange is going on, too? Could Alice be right about aliens being involved?"

"Woof, woof."

"Whoever that man was, he didn't want us poking around. Which makes me all the more determined to do so." A ping of worry hit me in the gut. What if he carried through with his threat to come after my loved ones?

Rather than feeling scared, I got angry. It wasn't fair what he'd done. He was wrong to threaten me. He was also very wrong to thump me over the head.

I stood carefully, my knees already less shaky thanks to the hot chocolate, and checked my reflection in the mirror. I had mud smeared on one cheek, and a large egg-shaped lump on my temple. I touched it and winced.

"We need to call in the big guns on this, Meatball. As amazing as you are, some muscle is needed." I dug my cell phone out of my pocket and sent a message to Campbell.

I could do with your help. Been attacked by a man in black.

The response was instant. *Are you hurt? Where are you?*

I've got a sore head. I'm back in my apartment.

I'll be there in two minutes.

I hadn't expected him to come right away, but I was glad. I really didn't want to be on my own.

I heated more milk and was mixing up hot chocolate for Campbell when there was a thudding on the front door.

I opened it, and he charged in. He grabbed my shoulders. His intense gaze ran over me, settling on the lump on my head. "Tell me everything. Who did this?"

"Slow down. Don't go all alpha male on me. I don't exactly know who did it."

"It's my job to go all alpha male in situations like this. Talk."

"I … I think whoever did this is worried I may uncover something. The attack could be linked to Adam's murder. The guy who hit me said something about keeping the past hidden."

Campbell growled and stared at the lump on my head.

"Take a seat. You're making me nervous. I've made you hot chocolate."

He released his hold on me after another careful inspection of my head injury. "Do you have blurry vision?"

"No, I don't think I have a concussion."

"If you feel sick or suddenly tired, go straight to the hospital. Actually, tell me, and I'll drive you there."

"I felt a bit sick when I first came to, but I think that was the shock more than anything. Please, I'll be okay. I need to talk this through with someone while it's fresh in my head."

"Your damaged head." Campbell checked the door was locked before going round and doing the same with the windows.

"I've already done that. No one's getting in."

"They could get in easily if they wanted to." He finally settled at the table and accepted a mug of hot chocolate from me. "So, spill. What happened?"

I topped up my own hot chocolate, grabbed a tin of cookies, and sat opposite Campbell. "I was out walking Meatball, when I met Bruce."

"Bruce Jonas is in the woods?"

"I think he's been hiding there. He was freaked out. He was certain someone was following him. He jumped at every tiny noise."

"Maybe the guy who got you was actually after Bruce."

"He could have been. I tried to convince Bruce to talk to the police, tell them what happened at Marchwood Manor, but he got scared. He ran off before I could get any more information out of him. But I did get something useful. He lied about his alibi."

"What did he tell you?"

"That he was with Jacob when Adam died. But he wasn't. Jacob was outside the house with Rupert and Dexter. Bruce wasn't there, I'm certain of it. Unless you saw him."

"No, he wasn't outside."

"Which means, he didn't tell the truth. So, what was he really doing that night?"

"I would have said he was pushing Adam off the veranda, but now this mysterious guy has turned up, it adds to the conspiracy cover-up. You didn't recognize him?"

"I didn't see him. He grabbed me from behind. He wanted me to stop poking around, and he threatened my friends and family."

Campbell growled low in his throat. "That's not acceptable. You're friends with Princess Alice and Lord Rupert. If that guy goes after them, he'll be in a world of hurt. I don't care which agency he's from, or how high up the chain of command this goes. The family must stay safe."

"I agree. He can't get away with this."

He gave a sharp nod. "Did you notice anything about him?"

I closed my eyes. "He smelled of peppermint, and maybe very faintly of whiskey. He also sounded very British. I mean, he had the kind of accent that would fit in anywhere while making you think he was posh. He had no trace of a regional dialect. And he was strong."

"Why did he hit you?"

"He shoved me away, and I turned to confront him. I was angry when he threatened other people, and I was worried he might hurt Meatball. I guess he didn't want me to see his face."

"You never hit a woman," Campbell said. "That's a coward's move. Especially not someone without any skills."

"Hey! I have skills."

"What can you do, beat someone to death with a whisk?"

"I'll give it a try on you if you keep being rude."

A smile traced across Campbell's face, but the worry behind it only made me nervous.

"What if he's still out there?" I said.

"I've got a team on their way to search the woods. Tell me where you were when you met him. That will speed things up."

I gave Campbell details of the walking route I'd taken with Meatball, and he sent them through to his team.

"You may find evidence that Bruce is out there as well. He said the churchyard is no longer safe, so he could be living in the woods full time," I said.

"They'll look out for him," Campbell said.

I finished my hot chocolate and picked up a cookie. "I really thought this was a simple case of Bruce killing Adam. Now this mysterious man has shown up, it's given me doubts."

"You're thinking about the aliens again?"

"No, not aliens. But it doesn't help that you're buying into the whole conspiracy theory idea."

"I'm looking at every angle," Campbell said.

I ate my cookie. "What if Bruce is involved in this cover-up? Didn't you say he was into science? Perhaps he worked at the testing lab."

"From the information I've dug up about him, which isn't much, he doesn't have a direct link to the facility. After he graduated from university, he went into the field of genetic manipulation. He worked at two places before he gave up his position because of his ill health."

"Genetic manipulation? Can you use that in viral weapons?"

"Sure. Biotechnology has been around since the Second World War. There are viral weapons that target people with specific genetic profiles. It's no stretch to imagine Bruce could have worked on a project like that."

I shuddered. "Why would anyone want to get involved in that sort of work?"

"Power, influence, money. Bruce received several large payments into his bank account early on in his career."

"Money from the testing lab?"

"I don't know. I haven't had any luck in tracing who paid that money in, which makes it unlikely to be from an honest source. But with his knowledge and expertise, it's likely Bruce picked up contract or freelance work along the way."

"Maybe one of those freelance jobs was working at this virus testing facility," I said. "What if he got involved in something there and things went wrong? Maybe Bruce is involved in this cover-up and Adam found out. It would give him a great motive for killing him."

"It would. I've managed to get access to Bruce's medical records. He was already taking antipsychotic drugs before he graduated university. He had a stable period for a few years, which was when those large payments appeared, then his prescription changed, which suggests he was no longer managing."

"Maybe he was struggling with the ethics side of his work. It could have affected his mental health. Genetic manipulation treads a fine line when it comes to what's acceptable."

"It does. I'll keep digging, see if I can find the source of those payments. If they track back to the virus lab, then we've got a direct link. Bruce killed Adam to cover up his connection to the work. He was ashamed of his past. A past Adam could have uncovered."

"So no aliens or government cover-up?" I said.

"It's still on the table. Although the space men aren't in the running."

Approaching footsteps outside the apartment had me tensing.

Campbell was on his feet and heading to the door. "Stay where you are."

"I'm not going anywhere," I said.

There was a rapid knocking. "Holly, it's Alice. Are you there?"

"I'm here, too," Rupert called out.

Campbell glanced at me. "We shouldn't involve them."

I bit my bottom lip. "They're already involved. Alice insisted on going to the churchyard to talk to Bruce today. Maybe she found out something useful."

"Holly! Let us in. What are you doing in there? I hear voices." Alice rapped on the door again.

Campbell pulled it open. "Good evening, Princess Alice."

"Oh! What are you doing here?" Alice glanced past him, and her eyes widened. "What happened to you?" She barged past Campbell and ran over to me.

"I got hit on the head," I said.

"Who hit you?" Alice frowned. "Tell me their name, and I'll make them sorry."

Campbell shook his head. "I'm looking into it, Princess."

"Oh! Yes, of course. Very good, Campbell." Alice fussed around me.

Rupert joined her. "You should see the doctor. I'll phone our family physician right away."

"No, there's no need. I feel okay," I said. "Why are you here? It's getting late. Did you find out something from Bruce?"

Alice's hand went to her mouth, and she glanced at Rupert. "Maybe we shouldn't worry you. Not if you've been hurt."

"Worry me about what?" I sat up straight in my seat.

"It's Bruce Jonas," Rupert said. "He's dead."

Chapter 12

I jerked back in my seat and stared up at Alice and Rupert. "Bruce is dead! But I only saw him a few hours ago. What happened?"

"We're not certain," Rupert said. "It was hard to see what was going on. He's definitely dead, though."

Campbell was talking on his cell phone. He ended the call and turned to us. "I've got the information. I'm heading to the scene now."

"We're coming, too," Alice said. "Oh! Only if you're up to it, Holly."

I was already on my feet and pulling my jacket back on. "Of course. The last time I saw Bruce, he was upset and stressed. And he was convinced someone was after him. They must have found him."

"Oh, no. Nobody killed him," Alice said as she followed me to the door with the others. "Apparently, it was a drug overdose. He even left a note. It looks like a suicide."

I looked over at Campbell and saw the disbelief written across his face. "Are you certain?"

"No, we're not. Alice is making assumptions. We couldn't get a good look at what was going on," Rupert said. "The police were there, but we overheard half a conversation about drugs and a note."

"Bruce is in the churchyard," Campbell said. "I can find out what's happening, but we need to leave now."

"Did you speak to him today?" I was glad Alice kept a tight hold of my arm as we left my apartment. I still felt wobbly as we hurried to Campbell's SUV.

"No! I had my dress fitting in the village—"

"Which took ages," Rupert said. "We wasted loads of time."

"It's never a waste of time to create something beautiful. And I don't know why you're complaining, you were served free champagne while you sat there doing nothing."

"It would have been rude to decline the offer." He glanced at me, looking a bit shamefaced.

"Anyway, after my fitting, we spent a couple of hours walking around looking for Bruce. I even got a blister on one heel," Alice said.

"Because you didn't wear the right shoes," Rupert said.

"Shush. We couldn't find him anywhere," Alice said. "We asked everyone we saw if they'd seen him, but he'd disappeared."

"I found him in the woods when I took Meatball for his evening walk," I said. "Bruce wasn't living in the churchyard, anymore. He got scared away."

We climbed into the SUV, and Campbell shot along the driveway and out onto the main road.

"Scared away by what?" Alice asked.

"Or who?" Rupert said.

I didn't miss the sharp glare Campbell gave me in the rearview mirror. "I'm not certain. It could be his paranoia making him act out."

Alice pinched my arm. "Or you could be hiding things. Don't tell me you're shutting me out and only working with Campbell. That's not fair. I'm your best friend. We share everything."

"Maybe that's why she's doing it, Princess." Campbell's hands were clenched around the steering wheel as we shot along the lanes at an alarming speed. "Holly wants to make sure you remain safe. We all do."

Alice waved a hand in the air. "That's what I've got you for and the rest of your security team. If I do anything foolish, you're on hand to sort things out."

A muscle clenched in Campbell's jaw, but he didn't reply.

A couple of minutes later, we arrived at the churchyard. There were two police cars, an ambulance, and a sleek black BMW parked outside.

I spotted Jacob, Dexter, Clive, and several other onlookers standing by the wall of the church.

We hurried over to join them, while Campbell diverted into the churchyard, heading to the open door of the church.

Jacob turned as we approached, his expression tight and his eyes damp. "Oh! Hi. You don't need to see this. It's Bruce. He's ... dead."

"Do you know what happened?" I asked.

Jacob said. "We're not sure. The police are saying it's drug related."

"Do they think he took an overdose?"

"He wouldn't do that," Dexter said, his attention on the church. "Bruce hated drugs. He never touched them."

"He rarely even drank," Jacob said. "I don't understand. There's also talk that he left a note. Someone even mentioned suicide."

Clive turned at the mention of suicide. He shook his head. "I hope it's not that. You never get over something like that. Bruce was a young man. He shouldn't have had to take his own life. He could have gotten help."

I felt sorry for Clive. This must bring up memories of what happened to his daughter. "Perhaps it's not a suicide."

"If it's not suicide, it has to be another murder," Dexter said. "In which case, this isn't a safe place to be. What kind of nightmare place is your father living in, Jacob?"

"We don't have murderers running around Audley St. Mary," Jacob said. "Dad chose this place because it's such a sleepy backwater. It's not so different from Appledore. He just wanted more space to host his parties and not disturb the neighbors."

"We sometimes get a bit of trouble," I said. "But it's not usually drug related."

"It can't be drugs," Jacob said. "That's out of character for Bruce. He always said he needed a clear head to take his pictures and recordings."

"He has been going downhill recently," Dexter said. "Maybe he couldn't handle his illness, anymore. He needed a way out."

"Do you know what he said in the note?" I said.

Jacob glanced at me. "You seem interested in this. I didn't know you and Bruce were close."

"I liked Bruce. I'd like to know what happened to him."

"So would all of us," Dexter said. "I hope this has nothing to do with what happened at the party."

"You mean, Adam's death?" I said.

"Oh! No, I wasn't thinking about that." Dexter lifted one shoulder and turned back to the churchyard. "I'd had too much to drink. Bruce was being particularly erratic. He got on my nerves. Normally, I'm more tolerant of him, but he kept saying the place wasn't safe and we had to check for bugs. It was ridiculous. And I, well, I yelled at him. I told him that he needed to pull himself together."

"Dexter, that was uncool," Jacob said. "You know what Bruce was like."

"It's not my proudest moment. But I hadn't seen him in ages. You're used to him. He was always hanging around your place in Appledore, then he drifted over this way when you moved. I didn't realize how bad he was. I messed up. I regret it. He always was a sensitive guy, even before his mental health problems."

"That's true," Clive said. "I worried about him when he was a kid. It can be a tough old world. He always picked up on people's struggles and wanted to help them."

"Bruce was an empath," Alice said. "He tuned into how other people felt. Like an emotional sponge."

"I don't know anything about that," Clive said, "but he was a fragile guy. Just like my Eleanor."

Dexter scrubbed a hand down his face. "I hope my fight with him didn't tip him over the edge. I'll never forgive myself if he did this because of me."

"I'm sure he didn't," I said. "He sounds like he was a clever guy. He would have understood you didn't mean it."

"Bruce was a full-on genius," Jacob said. "Always on the cutting edge. He had this way of looking at new innovations in other industries and applying it to science. Most of what he told me about his work went over my head. I have him to thank for getting me through science. I'd have flunked out if it hadn't been for him."

"I can't believe he's gone." Dexter clapped a hand on Jacob's shoulder.

"You were all friends because of the conspiracy gang?" I said.

Jacob and Dexter exchanged a glance.

Jacob nodded. "That's right. It was nothing serious, just a way to kill the time in boring old Appledore. It used to be fun, hanging out at disused buildings and making up stories about the things that happened there. I didn't believe any of it."

"Same here." Dexter pulled a hip flask from his jacket pocket and took a long drink. "It was a chance to get drunk and convince one of the girls to make out with me."

"What about the lab in Appledore you visited?" I said. "That sounds fascinating."

"It was boring, from what I remember," Jacob said, his attention fixed on the churchyard. "Nothing much going on there."

"I've seen pictures. What was with all the high fences and barbed wire?" I said.

Jacob shot me a sideways glare. "I don't remember that. Are you sure you're thinking about the same place?"

"Yes, in the trees, near the reservoir. I've heard all kinds of theories about what went on there, from food testing to virus creation."

"I remember us going there one night," Dexter said. "It was a waste of time. There was nothing to see, and we couldn't get inside most of the building. We had a poke around the fence, set off a couple of security lights, so legged it back into the forest."

"Did you see any guards while you were there?" I said.

Dexter rubbed the back of his neck. "There could have been. It was a long time ago. Why the interest in that place? I only mentioned it at the party as a joke."

I looked back at the churchyard. "It was something Bruce said to me. He was worried people were after him. I wondered if he'd worked at that site and gotten in some kind of trouble, especially if he was testing viruses."

"I don't think he ever worked there," Jacob said. "He was the one always obsessed with the alien conspiracy theories and finding us places to visit. Actually, Bruce and Adam were really into it. It was funny, Bruce was this big science geek, always studying and talking about new theories. Adam was a jock. Those two clicked over the conspiracy theory nonsense. I never really got it. Like Dexter, I was happy just to go along for the ride."

"Plus, there was nothing else to do around Appledore when we were growing up," Dexter said.

I was silent as I digested everything they'd told me. Had Bruce committed suicide because he felt so guilty about killing Adam?

"What about the rest of your group?" I said. "Were they into conspiracy theories as much as Bruce and Adam?"

Another look passed between the men. "I think they came along because they were bored, too. Eleanor was into the conspiracy theories, though. Isn't that right, Clive?"

Clive nodded. "She always had a vivid imagination. I don't know where she got it from. She even asked for books on conspiracy theories as presents. I indulged her. Maybe I shouldn't have. She always had her head in the clouds."

"That's a good thing," I said. "It's good to have a healthy imagination."

"It wasn't for Eleanor," Clive said. "Maybe if she'd been grounded in reality, she wouldn't have taken her split with Adam so badly. She could still be here." He ducked his head and shoved his hands into his pockets.

Dexter shuffled his feet and nodded.

Jacob patted Clive on the back. "You're doing okay, though, aren't you, Clive? I mean, we all miss Eleanor."

"I'm getting by, son. That's as good as it gets some days."

"We should leave," Dexter said. "It looks a bit creepy us lurking around outside the churchyard. We can't do anything to help Bruce now."

"Yeah, we should go," Jacob said. "I'll get an update from Dad's security when they know more. And we need to get back and tell Dad what's going on."

They both said a swift goodbye and hurried away.

A few seconds later, Campbell strode over. He looked around the group and frowned. "Holly, a word in private."

Alice squeaked. "No! That's not fair. Stop shutting us out."

"I promise, I won't hide anything from you," I said. "Just give us a minute."

"Let them talk." Rupert caught hold of his sister's arm. "Campbell knows what he's doing."

Alice huffed. "Don't be long. And you have to tell us everything."

I hurried away with Campbell and stood under the wooden arch leading into the churchyard. "What did you find out?"

"We have a problem."

"Bruce didn't die because of a drug overdose?"

"There were drugs involved, but I don't think he used them on himself. From what I saw at the scene, Bruce was killed. This was staged to look like a suicide."

Chapter 13

I grabbed the low stone wall to stay standing, shock reverberating through me. "Another murder. How can you tell Bruce was killed?"

Campbell glanced over his shoulder. "I have to be quick. I got word that Lee's in the area, and Marchwood Manor is patron to this church. He'll use that to claim jurisdiction and throw me out."

"Okay, so talk."

"The drug used was heroin."

"I don't know much about drugs. How can you tell Bruce didn't take it voluntarily?"

"There are puncture marks on his arms, but no needles. If Bruce injected himself with a large amount of heroin, the overdose would have been instantaneous. There'd have been no way he could have gotten rid of the needle."

"Someone injected him and then took the needle away?"

"Maybe they were worried they'd leave fingerprint evidence behind if they left the needle in his arm," Campbell said. "There are two injection sites. Whoever used the drugs on Bruce wanted to make sure he wouldn't survive."

"So, someone set this up. And someone not too smart if they left clues that this couldn't be a suicide."

"Or they got disturbed. They could have heard a noise and got scared off."

I looked up as a car drove past. Jacob was at the wheel, and Dexter sat beside him. "I was thinking Bruce killed Adam and then killed himself because he was so full of remorse."

"It can't have happened that way. This was no suicide."

"Could someone be picking off members of the conspiracy gang? First Adam, now Bruce. They were members of that group."

Campbell stared at the brake lights on Jacob's car as they flashed red. "Which means the others are at risk."

I blew out a breath. I'd tried to ignore the idea that a conspiracy cover-up was behind these deaths, but Bruce's murder only lent weight to the possibility. "If these murders relate to something the group uncovered, then Eleanor's death could also be connected. She died ten years ago after learning about the testing facility. Everyone said it was a suicide. What if it wasn't? Maybe it was a set-up, just like Bruce. Did she also die from a drug overdose?"

Campbell was quiet for a moment. I could imagine the cogs turning in his head. "I'll pull her file and take a look."

"What are you doing here?" Lee appeared out of the gloom, his expression tight as he strode over.

"I heard about the death and came to take a look," Campbell said.

"More like you're sticking your nose in where it's not wanted," Lee said. "You and your girlfriend need to leave right away."

Rather than arguing, Campbell simply nodded. "Good idea."

Lee blinked, surprise flashing across his face. "Go on then. Marchwood Manor looks after the church and the grounds. I'm in charge here. I need to see what mess the local police have made of things." He turned and marched away.

"Don't you want to get a proper look round before we leave?" I said. "There could be people who saw something useful."

"I've seen everything I need. I'm friendly with the local copper looking after the scene. He let me have a good look at the body. I told them to do a thorough search for any needle just in case it was thrown away by the killer when they ran, but I bet they don't find anything."

"What's our next move?" I gestured Alice and Rupert to catch up with us as Campbell walked back to his SUV.

"What's going on?" Alice said.

"Campbell thinks Bruce was murdered," I said.

"Oh! That's terrible." Alice clutched Rupert's arm. "Who would do such a thing?"

"We need to start at the beginning and be methodical," Campbell said. "Holly, you have to get into Marchwood Manor, then sneak me in so I can look at the scene of Adam's death. Lee is putting up too many barriers, and I haven't been able to look at the crime scene."

"Why me? Lee won't help me. He knows we work together."

"I'll help with that problem," Alice said. "Despite the fact you're leaving me out, I can get us into Marchwood Manor. It won't look strange if I pay a visit to a neighbor to see how they're getting along after the terrible accident. I can take Holly with me as my assistant."

"Princess Alice, you shouldn't be involved in this," Campbell said.

"It would be an easy way for us to get inside," I said.

"You see, I can be useful," Alice said. "Holly, you make something delicious for us to take to the Marchwoods. A sympathy cake, or something like that. That'll get us in. Then I can distract Sir Richard, Jacob, and anyone else who's around, while you two get to work finding the clues and stopping this dreadful killer from getting to anyone else."

"Only if it's safe," Rupert said. "Holly shouldn't be put at risk. She's already had a nasty fright this evening."

"I'm okay, and I was more angry than anything else. We have to get to the bottom of this," I said. "The killer staged Bruce's death to look like a suicide, but it was a clumsy attempt. They're killing for a reason, and we have to find out what it is, before they strike again."

Alice's hand went to her throat. "What's happened to our lovely village? Campbell, you must deal with this right away."

"It's too late to do anything tonight," I said. "I'll get baking first thing in the morning, then we can head over to Marchwood Manor together."

Campbell grumbled under his breath before nodding. "We do need to get inside to see if these murders are linked. If Lee hasn't joined the dots, and I'd place good money that he hasn't, he won't be linking Adam and Bruce's deaths."

"And I bet he won't be considering the possibility that Eleanor's supposed suicide could also be linked to these murders," I said.

"Then it's settled," Alice said. "We'll meet tomorrow at eight-thirty. You can take us over there, Campbell. You'll be my security detail and Holly will be my assistant."

"What will I be?" Rupert said.

Alice tutted. "If you must come with us, you can be my annoying older brother."

With a careful eye and a practiced hand, I swirled the piping bag over the chocolate coffee triple layer cake, finishing it with a thick layer of mocha cream and a grating of dark chocolate.

I'd been up early, not able to sleep since the discovery of Bruce's body in the churchyard.

I felt like I was being pulled in two directions. Firstly, there was the odd conspiracy gang link between the two victims, or possibly three victims, if Eleanor Carrell was included in this puzzle. They'd all been a part of the conspiracy gang when they were young.

There was also the unwelcome visit by the peppermint and whiskey breathed man in the woods, warning me off. That had to be linked to something the conspiracy gang had uncovered. But why now? Maybe they weren't even aware of the information they'd discovered, but someone was being extra careful. Who that someone was, I had no idea.

Secondly, and this seemed the more logical route to me, these murders happened because of a fight or grudge that got out of hand. This was the theory I preferred, but it seemed like I was in the minority.

I stepped back and surveyed the cake before adding a little extra chocolate.

Governments didn't go around bumping off people who got in their way. At least, not where I came from.

Maybe I needed to open my eyes. I lived a sheltered life, nestled in the beauty of Audley St. Mary and privileged to enjoy a lifestyle living in the castle grounds. Sometimes, life wasn't all delicious cakes and having fun. There was a grittier underbelly, one I sometimes stumbled across.

"But a conspiracy theory and a government cover-up?" I set my chocolate shaver down and shook my head. "There has to be another reason Adam and Bruce were killed."

Campbell strode into the kitchen. "Morning, Holmes. Nice cake. You ready?"

"Yes. I just need to find something to put this cake in."

"Princess Alice sent word to Sir Richard and Jacob that we're going to visit them this morning."

"I know. She sent me a message last night to say it was happening. Although I thought you'd have found a way to stop her being involved." I pulled out an empty cake tin from the cupboard and carefully set the cake inside before sealing the lid.

He grunted. "Don't think I didn't try. Every reason I came up with for her to stay out of this, she rebuffed. She resorted to threats and said she'd send me to the castle dungeon if I kept going against her instructions."

I chuckled. "I wouldn't put it past her to do something like that. Alice has a ruthless side."

"Which I've seen many times when she doesn't get her own way. And she'll need that ruthless side if she gets herself mixed up in this."

"You're still thinking this is a big government cover-up?"

"Maybe. Are you?"

"I'm thinking it's unlikely, but there's something behind it."

He snuck open the fridge and took out a cheese and ham croissant. "Come on, Princess Alice and Lord Rupert are waiting for us in the car."

I collected the chocolate coffee cake, made sure Meatball was happy in his kennel with plenty of treats and toys, and hurried out to the waiting SUV.

Alice was practically bouncing in her seat, a big smile on her face as I pulled open the door. "Get a move on. We don't want to be late. Cake for breakfast and two murders to solve. What a treat."

"I didn't think we'd have this cake for breakfast." I hopped in, and we were soon on our way to Marchwood Manor.

"Of course we can. Oh, unless Jacob isn't a cake person, which makes him horrible, and he's definitely not that. I'd have cake every day if my waistline would allow."

"Perhaps he'll offer us breakfast, instead. You love breakfast food," I said.

"So long as it isn't fruit. That's not a real breakfast. I'll suggest the cake as an option," Alice said.

"How about you remember your upbringing and don't insist on having things when you're in someone else's house," Rupert said.

"Oh, hush. You're no fun first thing in the morning," Alice said.

"You came in my room and jumped on my bed at six o'clock! How am I expected to be cheery when you invade my sleep?" Rupert yawned loudly. "Excuse me, Holly."

"No problem," I said. "Have you thought about what you're going to talk about when you see Jacob and Sir Richard?"

"I'll think of something," Alice said. "If all else fails, we can always talk about the weather."

Rupert tugged at his shirt collar. "Should we bring up the murders?"

"Definitely. It's sure to be a topic of conversation," I said. "Jacob must be upset over losing two friends in such a short space of time."

"And he's possibly feeling guilty," Alice said. "After all, wasn't it his idea to have the party?"

"You don't think he brought everyone together for that reason?" Rupert said.

"I can't see how that would work," Alice said. "Why would he invite his old school friends together just to kill them?"

"That's what we need to find out," I said. "But Jacob can't be involved in Adam's death. He was outside the house when Adam was pushed off the veranda."

"Jacob could have paid someone to do it," Alice said. "The Marchwoods are rolling in money. Campbell, how easy is it to hire an assassin?"

"Not as difficult as you may think, Princess."

"There you go, I've found something useful already. Is there anything in particular we need to look for when we're grilling Jacob?" Alice said.

"I'll be looking for the clues, Princess," Campbell said. "Your job is to distract everyone. I want to get a good look around the veranda for signs of a fight. Adam could even have been injured before he was pushed, so there could be DNA evidence."

"Blood, that sort of thing?" Alice's eyes sparkled.

"Exactly that," Campbell said.

"I'll come with you," I said to Campbell.

"No, I want you to stay with Princess Alice and Lord Rupert."

"To make sure we don't get in any trouble?" Alice giggled. "Don't you trust us, Campbell?"

"He knows you too well," I said. "It would be good to talk to Jacob about Bruce and Adam, see if we can find out anything useful."

"Then it's sorted. The three of us will ask the questions, while Campbell can employ his skills in finding clues. You never know. There could be an alien spaceship hidden on the veranda. That's something worth killing for," Alice said.

"We shouldn't mention aliens when we're asking questions. It'll make us look odd," I said.

"I'm not ashamed of my interest in aliens. You're the one with the closed mind when it comes to what goes on among the stars," Alice said.

I pressed my lips together and decided not to argue the point.

We arrived at Marchwood Manor and climbed out of the SUV.

The front door was opened by the head housekeeper who showed us into a bright, high-ceilinged parlor.

"I'll wait until Jacob comes in, then make my excuses," Campbell said. "I'll pretend to receive a call that needs my attention. I'll slip out of the room, and the rest of you keep everyone talking."

"Are you sure you don't want me to come with you?" I said. "Two pairs of eyes are better than one. And I'm good at spotting things."

He looked pointedly at Alice and Rupert. "Stay here. Keep an eye on things. Don't forget, we're hunting a killer. He could even be in this house."

I hated missing out on the chance to find clues, but Campbell was right. And as feisty as Alice could be, I didn't want to put her at risk. "Okay, I'll stay here. Tell me everything you find, though."

The door to the parlor opened. Jacob came in, his hair looking messy, as if it hadn't been brushed. "What a welcome party! It was a surprise to hear you'd be joining us this morning."

Alice hurried over and grasped his hand. "We wanted to see how you're doing. After what happened with Adam and your friend Bruce, you must be in shock. Such horrible tragedies." She led him over to the seats.

Jacob nodded a greeting at all of us. "Of course. It was terrible news. When I first woke up this morning, I thought it was a nightmare." He settled in a seat.

"Would you like some cake?" Alice gestured at the tin I held. "Holly made it especially for you."

Jacob's nose crinkled. "I'm not really into cake for breakfast. I'll ring for coffee."

Alice just about repressed a sigh. "It's very good."

Jacob settled back in his seat. "I've no doubt. I always make sure to enjoy a slice or two when I visit the castle. Bruce loved your cake, too." He glanced at me before his head lowered.

"Do you have your security team looking into what happened to Bruce?" I said.

"Yes, they were there last night at the churchyard, along with the police."

"And it was definitely drugs that did him in?" Rupert said.

"It must have been. It's the strangest thing, though. The police keep coming back to the problem of the missing needle," Jacob said.

I didn't miss the quiet huff of approval Campbell made.

"What missing needle?" I asked.

"They think it was heroin Bruce took, which I can't believe. He never touched the stuff. Anyway, they think he injected it. There was evidence on his arms, but there was no needle by his body."

"Do you think he was using with somebody else?" I said. "Perhaps he'd fallen in with a rough crowd. They could have taken the needle out of his arm."

"I suppose it's possible. I still can't believe that's how Bruce died. I always worried about him. He worked so hard to fit in, but it was a struggle. He must have been more desperate than I realized. I should have paid him more attention."

"Excuse me, Princess Alice, Lord Rupert. I've received a message I need to deal with." Campbell stood formally by the side of the couch.

"Of course," Alice said. "Off you go. You know where we are. We're perfectly safe inside the parlor."

Campbell opened the door and stood back to allow a server in with a full tray. She set it down and poured out coffee for us all before leaving.

"This whole business has gotten me shaken up," Jacob said.

"Is your other friend still here?" I said. "You're not on your own?"

"Yes, Dexter's staying until everything is figured out. I said he could stay as long as he liked. Dad's got plenty of rooms to fill."

"Where is Sir Richard this morning?" Alice asked. "Perhaps he'd like cake for breakfast."

"Of course, I forgot to say, he asked me to send his apologies. He had to go up to Cambridge on business," Jacob said. "He left early, before I was up."

"Oh, that's disappointing. I know Sir Richard loves Holly's cake," Alice said. Her gaze settled on the tin, and she sighed.

"You have some cake if you like," Jacob said.

"Oooh! Thanks. Don't mind if I do." Alice gestured at the tin. "Holly, cut it up."

"Um, I don't have a knife. And this is meant for Jacob." I arched my brows at her. She was getting distracted by her sweet tooth.

"That's no problem. I can find a knife." Jacob hopped up and left the room.

"Alice! You're not helping," I whispered.

"All I can smell is chocolate! If I don't have cake, I'll faint. You know I suffer from low blood sugar in the morning."

"You suffer from being greedy," Rupert said.

She glared at him. "So, you won't want any cake then?"

He shuffled in his seat. "I didn't say that. It does smell delicious."

I groaned. "Fine, you can both have cake. Just keep focused on what we're here to do."

Jacob returned with a knife and plates. "There we go. Mission accomplished." He settled in his seat.

I swiftly cut up two slices of cake and gave them to Alice and Rupert. I offered some to Jacob, but he declined.

"When I was at the party, there was mention of a couple of your old friends who couldn't make it," I said. "Have they been told what's happened to Adam and Bruce?"

"Actually, I haven't been in touch with them about that." Jacob stood and walked to the mantle. He returned with a picture in his hand. "This is all of us back in the good old days."

I studied the picture which showed a young-looking Jacob with short hair and a big grin, and a much more put together Bruce, who had a camera around his neck and was looking at something over his shoulder. There were also three girls and Dexter.

"The petite brunette in the middle is Eleanor," Jacob said. "The blonde is Emily Smithers, and the other brunette is Simone Matthews. It was Emily and Simone who couldn't make it to the party."

I peered at the picture. "You're all wearing wrist ties."

"Oh, yes! I'm surprised you noticed those. It was a silly thing, Adam's idea, actually. He wanted us to have some kind of branding for the conspiracy gang. We tossed around various ideas. At first, we were going for badges, but that seemed stupid. We thought about getting patches put on our jackets, but couldn't agree on a logo. Then it was suggested we get wrist ties. They were all the rage back then. We selected the colors, and Emily made them. Silly really, when you think about it."

"I think it's rather nice." Alice held her hand over her mouth as she ate cake. "It's good to have close friends when you're growing up."

"It was all the conspiracy stuff that brought us together," Jacob said. "Well, that and the stolen booze from our parents' drinks cabinets."

"Do any of you still look into conspiracy theories?" I asked.

"Yes! Tell us about anything you've found related to aliens," Alice said.

Jacob's forehead wrinkled. "I've got nothing for you. I don't bother with that these days. Bruce was always talking about strange things, though. Although that had more to do with his mental health than anything else. I can't tell you about Simone or Emily. In fact, I haven't got a clue what happened to Simone. I haven't seen or heard anything about her in almost ten years."

"Was there a falling out in the group?" Alice said.

"Nothing like that. It was all a bit odd. It was just after Eleanor's suicide. Simone and Eleanor were close. I think the suicide badly affected her. She just left."

"When you say left, you mean she moved away from Appledore?" I said, recalling what Dexter had told me about Simone's disappearance.

"No. She literally vanished in the night. She took a few things, told her mom she was going away for a couple of weeks, and headed off. Simone was always the independent one in the gang, so it wasn't so weird for her to go off exploring. I kept dropping by her mom's house to see what was going on, but she was none the wiser. Then she got a note from her saying she'd gotten early acceptance into university in America and that she'd be in touch."

"America! That's quite an adventure," Alice said.

"Typical Simone. She never does anything by halves," Jacob said.

"Did you contact her at the university?" I said.

"I tried. I contacted the one she went to, but they had no record of her. I didn't want to worry her mom, so I didn't mention it, and she kept getting postcards from her so was happy enough. It meant Simone was safe wherever she was."

"What about the pretty blonde in the picture?" Alice was now studying the photograph.

"That's Emily Smithers. Up until recently, she worked as a psychiatrist. I sent her loads of messages to convince her to come to the party, but she ignored them until the last minute when she sent a brief note saying she couldn't come because of work commitments. She runs the practice, so I guess it's pretty hectic. It would have been great to catch up with her, though," Jacob said.

"Does she specialize in a particular kind of psychiatry?" Rupert asked.

"She's made a name for herself studying the long-term effects of drugs on mental health," Jacob said. "She's a hundred times smarter than me."

"It's a shame she wasn't around to help Bruce," Alice said.

"As much as I hate to say this, I think Bruce was past saving. He had so much help over the years, but every time he seemed to make a recovery, he'd slide back and things got worse."

"Maybe that's why Emily followed that particular specialism in psychiatry," I said. "She remembered an old friend who was suffering and thought she may be able to help him. Or if not him, other people with serious mental health conditions."

Jacob's smile was soft. "I'd like to think that was true, and she still remembered us. Emily's probably moved on by now. That must be why she decided not to come to the party. I haven't talked to her for a long time. People change. I know I'm not the same self-obsessed teenager I used to be. At least, I hope I'm not that self-obsessed. Teenage boys can be a horror, isn't that right, Rupert?"

A yell had me jumping to my feet. "That sounded like Campbell."

Alice joined me and we looked out the window. She gasped. "That doesn't look good."

I grimaced as I spotted Campbell and Lee.

Lee had a firm hold on Campbell's arm and was trying to shove him away from the house. Campbell wasn't budging.

I kept my voice low. "Come on, Alice. We have to deal with this before Campbell rips Lee's head off and our ruse gets discovered."

Chapter 14

"What's going on?" Jacob asked. He was on his feet, standing next to Rupert.

I dashed to the door of the parlor with Alice. "It looks like a misunderstanding between Lee and Campbell. We'll sort it."

"Hurry! We can't let Jacob overhear them arguing. Lee must have caught Campbell snooping. He could ruin everything," Alice whispered.

"I'm more worried about Campbell snapping Lee's neck," I said as we headed into the hallway. "They loathe each other."

"Perhaps I should order him to do just that," Alice said. "Lee is mean and rude."

"That's not a good idea, unless you want Campbell to go to jail."

"We could say it was self-defense. We'd back him up if he has to do something so deadly. We'll say Lee gave him no choice but to snap him like an after dinner mint."

"Alice! We need to stop this fight before it leads to another murder." I pulled open the main door and ran outside. I was faster than Alice because she was wearing kitten heels and we were running across gravel, so I quickly outpaced her.

"Hey! What are you two doing?" I said.

Campbell and Lee ignored me as they tussled. Lee had Campbell in a headlock, but it only lasted a second. Campbell flipped around, jabbed an elbow in Lee's kidney, and clamped him around the throat, holding him against his chest.

Lee made a gurgling sound and flailed his arms.

"Stop! Everyone in the house can see what you're doing. It doesn't look professional," I said. I stayed several paces back, just in case things turned deadly.

Campbell growled. "He almost pushed me off the veranda."

"Even so, it's best not to strangle him. Sir Richard wouldn't like it," I said.

"He's insane!" Lee gasped and twisted in Campbell's grip. "I'll have him arrested for breaking and entering."

"We were invited here," I said. "Campbell must have been checking on some security matter."

"I don't believe that. He was on the veranda. There's nothing up there." Lee wheezed and his face turned purple.

"Campbell, let Lee go. He won't do anything silly now there's an audience," I said.

"Don't be so sure of that. He hasn't got a brain cell in that thick skull." Campbell's muscles flexed around Lee's throat before he shoved him away.

Lee staggered, almost landing on the dirt. He righted himself at the last second and spun back to Campbell, his face beet red and his hands clenched.

Alice reached my side and gasped in a breath. "You could have waited for me. I missed all the fun."

"There's nothing to see," I said. "Just a misunderstanding that got out of hand."

"I didn't misunderstand anything." Lee rubbed his neck. "I caught Campbell snooping around the murder scene. Were you trying to hide evidence of your involvement?"

"You see. Not a brain cell in there," Campbell said.

"You're convinced Adam was murdered?" I said to Lee.

He glowered at me. "Not that it's any of your business, but yes, there's evidence he was pushed."

"What evidence?" Alice said. "You can tell us. We're on the same side."

"Whatever's going on out here?" Jacob hurried over with Rupert. "Lee, is there a problem?"

"No problem, sir. I caught the Audleys' security in a restricted part of the house. I was just escorting him off the premises. I can always call the police if you want him arrested for trespass."

"That's not a problem," Jacob said. "Dad's given the okay for Audley Castle security to work with us. I'm sure he was only looking around to see if he could help."

"There's no need to involve them, sir. Everything's under control," Lee said.

Jacob's expression hardened. "If that's the case, why did one of my friends die last night in the churchyard? There's something strange going on around here. It doesn't feel safe to me." He turned to Campbell. "I'm sorry if there was any confusion. Lee can be a bit hot-headed, but he's only doing his job."

I glanced at Lee. It looked like he was about to explode.

"There's no harm done," Campbell said. "I wanted to make sure nothing had been missed. We've experienced trouble at the castle in the past, so I'm happy to lend my expertise."

Jacob nodded. "Of course. And you're welcome here. If you need to see anything, just ask me. Ignore the security. All I care about is finding out what happened to Adam and Bruce." He turned back to Lee. "Share any information you have on both cases with Campbell. You heard him, he knows what he's talking about when it comes to murder."

"More like, you do," Alice whispered in my ear. "You always solve the murders before Campbell."

I nudged her with my elbow. "Let's keep that to ourselves for now. There's some serious testosterone flying about and we don't want to damage any fragile male egos."

"I've not been withholding anything, sir," Lee said. "The evidence on both cases is being processed."

"You could tell us about the evidence showing how Adam was killed," I said.

Lee's body stiffened. "That's under review."

"It's fine. And I can tell you about that," Jacob said. "I heard about it when Dad was debriefed by the police. Several pots had been knocked over on the veranda, suggesting there was a struggle. There were also scratch marks on the concrete, as if someone had held on to the ledge. The police reckon Adam was shoved over and grabbed the edge, but couldn't hang there for long."

"Maybe whoever pushed him, prized his fingers off the ledge," Alice said.

Jacob shuddered. "It doesn't bear thinking about, but it's a possibility. There was also blood up there. It's a match for Adam's. His fall was no accident."

"I'm so sorry to hear that, Jacob," I said. "If there's anything we can do to help, just ask."

He shook his head. "Thanks, but I'm not sure what you can do. I mean, obviously, if Campbell can look into things and make head or tail of this, that would be great."

"I've got good connections with the local police. I'll see what I can do to help." Campbell glanced at Lee.

Lee remained straight-backed. The only giveaway that he was raging mad was his chest heaving in and out.

"And you made me that wonderful cake," Jacob said. "Your baking always cheers me up, Holly."

"There's plenty more cake if you ever need it. You just drop by the castle kitchen whenever you need a sweet fix and I'll sort you out."

"Thanks." Jacob looked up at the veranda and shook his head. "I'd better get inside. Busy day. Thanks for dropping by, everyone."

We said our goodbyes and headed away from the manor house, leaving behind a glowering Lee.

"I thought you were going to throttle Lee," I said to Campbell as we climbed back into the SUV and drove away.

"I was tempted. I was looking around the veranda when he jumped me. He must have seen me go up the stairs and crept after me."

"You were so brave, fighting with him," Alice said. "Lee's a big man. Almost as big as you."

"He's no match for me, Princess."

"Of course not. We only hire the best at Audley Castle." Alice sat back in her seat. "What a useful morning. We now know Adam was definitely murdered, and the police are investigating Bruce's death. They think it's suspicious as well."

"And we learned from Jacob about his missing friends, Simone and Emily," I said.

"What did you find out about them?" Campbell said.

"Emily Smithers works in psychiatry and specializes in mental health and long-term drug use," I said. "She also refused all the invites to the party, and they haven't been in contact for a long time."

"Then there's the weirdness about Simone Matthews," Alice said. "She disappeared right after Eleanor's suicide. She left with barely anything and headed to America to go to university. Surely it's not that simple. You don't turn up in another country and go to school."

"I don't think it is. Everyone has to go through an application process to get a place at university. I imagine there are more restrictions in place if you want to study abroad. That seems suspect to me," I said.

Campbell grunted. His gaze met mine in the rearview mirror. The look was loaded. It suggested I keep quiet until we were on our own.

"I'll take you back to the castle," Campbell said to Rupert and Alice.

"I wouldn't mind a proper breakfast," Alice said. "Your cake was delicious, Holly, but I only ate a very small piece so Rupert wouldn't accuse me of being greedy."

"You actually had two slices," Rupert said. "I saw you sneak that second piece."

She smacked him on the arm. "I did not. Well, I had one proper slice of cake. It simply came in two tiny pieces. Two small pieces equals one regular slice."

"You still ate more than you should," Rupert said.

She rolled her eyes. "Holly, come and join us for breakfast. We can talk about the murders some more and figure out what to do next."

"I'd love to, but I need to get to work," I said. "I didn't get a chance to tidy my baking equipment before we left. Chef Heston won't be happy that things are a mess."

"Oh, very well. But let me know the second you hear anything new," Alice said.

"Of course. I'll catch up with you both later."

We arrived at the castle, and I climbed out of the SUV and waited with Campbell until Alice and Rupert had gone inside.

He stood facing the castle, his arms crossed over his chest. "This all fits. Eleanor's apparent suicide, Adam being murdered when the conspiracy gang got back together, Emily refusing to have anything to do with them, and Bruce's faked suicide."

"Someone's picking them off one by one, aren't they?"

"I reckon so. And I looked into Eleanor's death. It was drugs. An overdose."

"Just like Bruce. But why? What secret are they hiding that's worth killing for?"

"They must have found out something they shouldn't."

"Something? Like what? You think this has to do with a discovery the gang made all those years ago?"

"I do. And, add to that your encounter with the stranger in the woods. This ties back to something much bigger."

"I wish it was simply a case of murder because of someone's jealous husband. That kind of murder I can handle. This, I'm not so sure about."

"I bet you're regretting getting involved now."

I was. Big time. "Do you think I'm in any danger?"

"Probably."

I swallowed, my throat tight. "Maybe you can handle the rest of this investigation on your own. I mean, you've got the military background and training. Weren't you some black ops covert military expert?"

He snorted a laugh. "Something like that. You scared, Holmes?"

"Terrified. And you should be, too. Some secret government agency could be after us to keep this quiet. We won't stand a chance."

"You won't stand a chance. I'll be fine. I have plans if things go south."

"Go south! I don't even know what that means. What happens to me if there's trouble?"

"You run. Hide. Come out with your hands up. Or, I could use you as a diversion while I slip away to my new life working on a beach in the Caribbean."

I laughed. "You selling tropical drinks out of a coconut shell is something I have to see."

"You could try, but you'd most likely be dead."

My laughter died. "This is serious, isn't it?"

"Whatever they uncovered all those years ago is making waves, but we don't know what it is."

"Please don't let it be about aliens. Alice will never let me hear the end of it," I said.

"Governments cover up all kinds of things."

"You think this is about aliens, too?"

"I ... don't know."

"You aren't reassuring." I pressed a hand against my churning stomach. "You take over from now on."

He smirked. "You make it sound like you're in charge."

"No! I want out. Just let me know what happens at the end."

"You're always demanding you get involved in my cases. This time, you have no choice. You're involved whether you want to be or not."

"I don't want to go up against a government agency. I'm out of my depth."

"They'll only kill you if necessary."

I glared at him. "You'll be okay. You can fight your way out of any situation."

"I've seen how you handle a whisk. You could take out a few attackers if your back was against the wall. Just make sure you're prepared."

"Prepared for what?"

"Prepared for anything. As you've already discovered, you never know when they may strike."

"I'll need my own security detail at this rate."

"I can't help with that. I've got the family to keep an eye on. Look after yourself, Holmes." He flashed me a grin before walking away.

He was being deliberately mean. The one time I didn't want to help on a murder investigation, and Campbell was refusing to let me out of it. Anyone would think he wanted me dead.

∞∞∞∞ ∞∞∞∞

I grabbed my laptop during my lunch break and sat in the afternoon sunshine as I ate my smoked ham and sundried tomato toasted sandwich while researching Emily Smithers.

There were several pages detailing her experience and where she graduated. She'd published numerous academic papers in the field of psychiatry and seemed respected in her field.

"Excuse me. Do you mind if I sit with you?"

I looked up to see a slim, middle-aged woman wearing a baseball cap. She was holding a brown paper bag in her hand. "The café is crowded, and I'd rather like some peace while I eat my lunch."

"Oh, well this area isn't really for visitors to the castle." She must have wandered around here from the outdoor seating area.

"Please. I've got a headache, and there's nowhere to sit outside."

"Oh! Sure. I don't see why not? It's just me out here."

"Thanks. I'm not interrupting anything, am I?" She settled on the wooden bench opposite me and pulled out a cheese sandwich and a can of drink.

"No, I'm killing time during my lunch break. I work in the kitchens at the castle."

"It's such a beautiful place to work. I'm jealous." She bit into her sandwich.

Meatball wandered over. He slowed as he spotted the woman and his hackles rose.

"Is that your dog?" she asked.

"Yes. He's friendly. Don't worry about him."

Meatball sat down, his gaze fixed on the woman.

"Ignore him if he's staring. He's only interested in your food. He doesn't need anything extra to eat, though."

"I used to have a dog just like that. He'd do anything for a chunk of cheese."

"Meatball is much the same," I said. "Are you enjoying your visit to the castle?"

"It's stunning. I can't believe a family still lives here."

"Yes, the Audley family. They're decent people to work for. The castle has been in their family for generations."

"Do you get to see much of them?"

"They're often around. The Duke and Duchess keep to themselves, and they're often away on civic duties. Princess Alice Audley and Lord Rupert Audley are always here, though."

"I wouldn't know whether to curtsy, or what to say if I ever met them," she said.

"They do sometimes do a walkabout when there are visitors here, so you never know, you may bump into them." The glint of the woman's wristwatch caught my eye. It looked expensive, possibly a Rolex.

"I was hoping to visit some other stately homes in the area. Are there any you can suggest?" she asked.

"There are lots of beautiful homes around here. You could start by taking a walk round the village green. There are plenty of old Tudor buildings to look at."

"I'd like something a bit grander. A big manor house, perhaps. I heard about Marchwood Manor. Is that nearby?"

"It is." My heart skipped a beat. "What have you heard about the place?"

"Oh, this and that. It sounds impressive."

I studied her more closely. I really couldn't tell what she looked like. She wore her dark baseball cap low, and I could just see a few strands of pale blonde hair sticking out. Her eyes were covered with large sunglasses. "Are you here with a coach touring party?"

"No, I came on my own. I don't like getting tied down if the group is particularly slow. This way, it gives me a chance to have a good look round and make sure I don't miss anything."

"I'm the same. I like to go off exploring on my own."

She finished her sandwich. "It's best if you don't explore too carefully. You never know what you could run into."

Meatball growled. His hackles were still raised. Was he picking up on a strange vibe? I know I was.

"What do you think I could run into?" I tried to keep my tone light, even though my heart was thudding.

"I've heard strange things about Audley St. Mary. And people stumble into all sorts of things they don't mean to. I even heard there was a murder here recently."

"Where did you hear that?" I lowered my laptop screen.

She shrugged. "I forget. Anyway, you need to back off."

My eyebrows shot up. "Back off of what?"

"And stop Campbell Milligan asking questions too if you care about his well-being."

I gripped the edge of the wooden bench. "How do you know Campbell?"

"I know a lot of things. I know about you, Holly Holmes. You're drawing too much attention to yourself. Stay out of this. It's old news. No one is interested in a disused food lab."

My eyelids fluttered. She was here to keep me quiet. "You've lost me. I don't—"

"If you keep on poking around, you'll only regret it."

No one threatened me, especially not when I was enjoying my favorite toasted sandwich and trying to relax in the sunshine. "You know what happened to Adam and Bruce, don't you?"

"I have no clue who you're talking about."

"You just mentioned a murder. Did you do something to Bruce?"

She lifted a shoulder. "You'll only find trouble if you keep on looking. This is a friendly warning. The next one won't be."

"What about Simone and Emily? Have you spoken to them and warned them to keep away? Is that why they didn't come to Jacob's party?"

"Those names mean nothing to me. And I know nothing about a party."

"You should know all about Emily and Simone. They were part of the group poking around the so-called disused food lab you're interested in me not knowing about."

She waved a hand in the air. "Kids were always doing that when the site was open. You throw up a high fence and some barbed wire and it's like flies around honey. Dumb kids will always poke around where they shouldn't."

"Why should you care if they poked around if you were just testing food? Surely, you'd have nothing to hide."

Her lips pressed together. She lowered her sunglasses a fraction and her cold blue gaze met mine. "You ask a lot of questions for a baker."

"And you know a lot for a tourist visiting Audley Castle."

We stared at each other.

Meatball kept softly growling.

"There you are! I was asking in the kitchen to see where you'd gotten to." Alice wandered out of the kitchen door, a plate of food in her hand. "Oh, and you're having lunch with a friend. Do I need to be jealous?"

The woman was already on her feet and walking away.

"Hey, we hadn't finished talking." I stood, uncertain whether to chase after her.

The woman ignored me and kept on walking.

"Was it something I said?" Alice sat on the bench. "Holly, are you okay? Your face is very red."

"No, I'm not okay. I don't know who that woman was, but she warned me about poking around in the murders."

Alice gasped. "Where's Campbell when you need him? He could have stopped her. Did she tell you why you should stop poking around?"

"I asked about the conspiracy gang, but she claimed to know nothing about them." I took a step in the direction the woman had gone, but stopped. Chasing after her was foolish. "We need to speak to someone else who was in that gang, see if they know what happened when they went to visit that lab."

"Who do you want to talk to? Shouldn't we tell the police this woman just threatened you?"

"If I tell the police, what will they do? I can't even give them a description, and she didn't hurt me."

"She threatened you. At least tell Campbell. The fact she's warning you off, means you're onto something. You've almost found our missing aliens."

"I'm still not sold on the alien theory."

"I am. You just wait." Alice jerked her head in the direction the woman had gone. "I wonder if the mystery woman knows anything about the aliens."

"Let's focus on what we already know. How would you like to go on a trip to visit a knitting group?"

"A knitting group? Why do you think they're involved? No one got stabbed with a knitting needle."

I opened my laptop and pointed at the screen. "Six months ago, Emily Smithers liked this knitting group on her social media page. We should go there and ask around, see if we can get a lead on her. She could have answers about what's going on."

"Count me in. Shall we go now?"

"I won't be able to get the afternoon off work. Tomorrow is my day off. We'll go first thing. Let's see if the knitters know anything about these murders."

Chapter 15

I eased the van to a stop by a crumbling brick wall. I tapped my fingers on the steering wheel, peering around for any sign of trouble. It could come in the form of Campbell, wondering what I was doing lurking by the castle wall, but I was also on high alert for any threats coming from supposedly friendly strangers.

A tap on the passenger side window made me jump. I opened the door, and Alice climbed in. "Did you have any problem getting away?"

"It was easy. The security team know I rarely get up early, so I just had to be extra quiet while I was sneaking around, before using the secret passages to get out. We'll head over to Cambridge, and I'll be back before they even know I've gone."

"We won't be long. The group meets at the Fluffy Ball of Yarn Café. It's on the edge of Cambridge." I kept checking my rearview mirror to make sure no one had seen us, but it looked like we'd gotten away with it.

Meatball shuffled onto Alice's lap and gave a yawn.

"He's not used to being up early either," Alice said. "I shall have to make up for these early starts by having an extra-long lie in soon. Or a vacation. I haven't been away for a while. Mommy and Daddy keep talking about taking me and Rupert to St. Kitts, but I like it here. And if I go away, I can't hang out with you."

"I'm honored. You're passing up the Caribbean to spend time with me."

"You're almost worth it. Oooh! Here's an idea. You could come with us."

"Chef Heston would love that."

"I could insist on it. Say I couldn't manage a single day without your amazing cakes."

"He'd definitely hate that. I think he gets jealous because you prefer my cakes over his. After all, he did study under the great pastry chef Gaston Lenôtre."

"His desserts are almost as good as yours. He beats you on the savories. Maybe I could bring you both along."

"Before we do any vacationing, we need to figure out what's going on with Adam and Bruce."

"It's a long shot, trying to track down Emily through this group you discovered."

"It's all we've got. She liked the Facebook page months ago. Maybe Emily likes to knit. She could go to the café to knit."

"I was never any good at knitting," Alice said. "I'm all fingers and thumbs. Let's hope this is the break we need."

It took about twenty minutes to drive to the café. I was glad we'd left early. The roads were still quiet, and it often got gridlocked around Cambridge, especially during peak tourist season when visitors flocked from all over the world to see the soaring spires and ancient colleges of the university.

I eased the van into a parking space close to the café, and we climbed out.

I slowed as I reached the door of the café. "We may have a problem."

"Don't tell me they're shut," Alice said.

"No, they're open. But I now get why the café is called The Fluffy Ball of Yarn Café. It's a cat café. Look, I can see several cats inside."

Alice clapped her hands together. "Even better. Cats, coffee, and cake. Perfection."

I looked down at Meatball. "If they let you in, you must be on your best behavior. Not every cat wants to be your friend."

He wagged his tail. Meatball was great around all animals, but he could get overexcited if a cat made a run for it.

"I'll hold him. He always behaves himself when he's with me." Alice scooped Meatball into her arms.

I opened the door and walked inside.

"I'll be right with you," a woman called from the back room.

The café was a mixture of calming green and blue hues. There were dozens of shelves, many lined with books about knitting or crochet and sewing patterns. The shelves had been designed so the cats could also use them. I spotted a dozen cats perched on the shelves. There were also several comfortable looking couches, and numerous cat beds and scratching poles dotted around.

"I've never been to a cat café," Alice said.

Meatball whined as he saw he was surrounded by cats and wriggled in Alice's arms.

She kissed the top of his head. "Be a good boy and they may play with you."

I picked up a leaflet from the table. "They're all rescue cats. What a nice thing to do, give them a foster home while they're looking for their forever home. They all look very content."

"I bet they get loads of cuddles from people coming into the café," Alice said. "What do you think, Meatball? Shall we adopt a few?"

"The Duchess's corgis will have something to say about that if you return home with an armful of kittens."

"It would do them good. The cats might put them in their place. Those dogs are terrors," Alice said.

"I'm sorry to keep you." A short woman with dark hair and a warm smile walked out the back room. "You're a bit early if you're here for the beginners knitting group."

"Oh, we're not here to knit," I said. "I'm Holly, and this is Alice. We're after some information about a friend of ours we haven't seen for a while. I think she comes here."

She nodded at us both. "I'm Sophie Duke. I own the place." Her gaze went to Meatball. "I hope he's not going to be any bother. I love all animals, but the cats come first. Some of them can be a bit nervous around noisy dogs."

"He's always good," I said. "And Alice will keep hold of him the whole time we're here."

"That's good enough for me," Sophie said. She scratched Meatball between the ears. "So, who are you looking for?"

"While we're here, why don't we have something to eat?" Alice said.

Sophie smiled. "We've got our breakfasts going at the moment. Take a look at the menu."

It was only polite to order something since we needed answers from Sophie.

"I'll have the breakfast scones and a pot of tea," I said.

"I'll have the same," Alice said.

"Anything for your dog?" Sophie asked.

"Any food would be appreciated," I said. "Or just a bowl of water."

"Take a seat. I should warn you, the cats often come over to say hello, especially if you have food. There are treats for them on the table. And they love attention, so feel free to give them plenty of strokes." Sophie petted a large white fluffy cat before heading back behind the counter.

"This is an amazing place." Alice settled at a small table and looked around. "And it's a charity. I'll make sure the castle adds them to their donation list and sends them some money."

"I'm sure they'd appreciate that," I said.

Alice leaned over and lifted up two knitting needles and a ball of wool. "Do you think it's okay if I have a go?"

"You're welcome to try." Sophie returned with our tea and Meatball's water. "Have you ever knitted before?"

"A long time ago. And I was dreadful. I don't have a knack for knitting."

"Everyone can learn. It just takes practice. I'll be back in a couple of minutes with your breakfast, and I'll show you how to get started." Sophie left us to it.

"She seems friendly." Alice peered at the knitting needles. "Do you think she'll help us with Emily?"

"So long as we don't say anything about conspiracy gangs, aliens, or murder, we should be okay. I don't want to alarm her."

"I won't mention any of that," Alice said. "We'll say we were friends and lost touch after school, something like that."

"That'll work." I smiled at Sophie as she returned with our breakfast scones. "You're welcome to join us."

"Well, I'm hardly rushed off my feet." She smiled as she looked around the café. "We'll be busy later. I've got three knitting groups booked in, and a dozen afternoon tea parties. People love having tea with our cats."

"I can see why. This is a great place," I said.

"Thanks. I work hard to make sure the cats have a good life." Sophie pulled out a chair and sat. "You were interested in finding a friend?"

"That's right. Emily Smithers. We know her from school, but we lost touch. I'm thinking of putting together a reunion party and wanted to find her. I know she's keen on knitting."

"I know Emily." Sophie smiled. "She's very sweet. And she does love to knit. I haven't seen her for a while, though."

"Does she still live around here?" I said.

"Not that I know of, but I can't imagine she'd travel too far. You can knit just about anywhere. I think she comes because she has such a stressful job. She told me once that she found it relaxing, losing herself in a pattern, while stroking some cats."

"Is Emily still working as a psychiatrist?" I asked.

"She never talks much about her job, but it's something science or medical related. I don't push her to find out more about her work. I think she comes here to get away from it."

A large, sleek Siamese cat strolled over. He placed his paws on Alice's knee and gave Meatball a thorough sniffing.

Meatball watched his every move, his whiskers bristling with excitement, but he stayed still.

"That's Arthur. He's king cat around here. Your little dog better be careful, Arthur can be a bit grumpy if he doesn't take to you," Sophie said.

Meatball tried to sniff Arthur. He backed away and hissed.

"I see what you mean," Alice said. "Meatball, maybe you'd like to play with the cute kitty."

"It's funny you should say that, we have a playpen in the corner. We put the cats in there if they need a time out. Some of them get overwhelmed with all the attention they get in the café when there are lots of customers. When they're in the playpen, they're out of bounds to the public. It gives them a time to relax. Cats need their space too."

"What do you think, Holly? Should we put Meatball and Arthur in the pen together?" Alice said.

"I trust him around cats. And he does love to play. We'll keep an eye on them, make sure the fur doesn't start flying," I said.

"It's just over there." Sophie caught hold of Arthur and lifted him onto her shoulder. "This is one clever cat. Don't be surprised if he runs rings around your dog."

Alice carried Meatball to the playpen and lowered him in. There were blankets, toys, and several scratching posts in there.

He trotted around and had a good sniff of everything, his tail wagging.

"Let's see how these two get on." Sophie lowered Arthur into the playpen.

He strutted around a bit, flicking his tail and ignoring Meatball.

Meatball couldn't resist and was soon trotting after Arthur, trying to get his attention.

"They look like they'll be fine," Sophie said. "Arthur's in charge."

I petted Meatball as he stopped to sniff a toy mouse. "Yep. Looks good."

"So, Emily. I'm not sure what else I can tell you about her," Sophie said.

"When was the last time you saw her?" I said. "I don't suppose she's booked on any of the groups today?"

"No, she isn't. It's been a few months. I figured her work had gotten too busy. Although she was talking about taking time off. I wondered if she'd gone away somewhere. She needed a break. She lives on her nerves."

"Do you have contact details for her?" I said. "It would be great to catch up and see if she could come to this reunion."

"No, I don't think I do. Most people interested in the café get in touch online. Give me a minute, I'll go and check my contacts book." Sophie hurried out the back again.

I stood with Alice, and we watched Arthur and Meatball running around together. Arthur occasionally fired off a warning hiss when Meatball got too boisterous, but other than that, they were getting along well.

"If we can't find Emily, I'm not sure what our next move should be," I said.

"Maybe Campbell will have some new clues to follow," Alice said.

"The trouble with him, is he's distracted by his rivalry with Lee."

"He'll still do a great job. I trust Campbell."

"So do I, but he's stuck on the government cover-up as the only option. What if we're looking at this wrong?"

"The aliens are out there?" She grabbed my arm. "What if the person who hit you in the woods was an alien in disguise?"

"An alien who drank whiskey?"

"It's possible. I'm sure they have sophisticated disguises. They've been walking among us for decades."

"I was hoping Emily would have an answer for us. She could put this whole conspiracy idea to bed."

"Or confirm it," Alice said.

Sophie returned to the playpen. "Sorry, I've got nothing that can help you find Emily. Maybe you could send her a message online. That's how she got in touch with me."

"Thanks. We'll try that," I said.

"While you finish your breakfast, why don't I show you how to get started with knitting, Alice?" Sophie said. "I'll even send you away with a beginners pack so you can have a go when you're home."

"That sounds perfect," Alice said. "I'm always looking to learn new skills."

The next half an hour was spent with Alice mastering the knitting basics under Sophie's patient tutelage, while I ate my scones and kept an eye on Meatball and Arthur.

The main door to the café opened and a group of half a dozen women came in, all clutching bulging bags full of knitting.

Sophie looked up and gave them a wave. "I won't be a minute, ladies. Sorry, that's my ten o'clock class. I hope you've enjoyed yourself. Do come back again."

"It's been great fun," Alice said. "Thanks so much. I'll definitely keep trying with the knitting."

We paid for our food and Alice's knitting pack, collected Meatball from the playpen, and headed outside.

"Well, we didn't get far finding out about Emily," I said.

"We did have a delicious breakfast, and I was able to knit a whole row. I could have a scarf done by the end of the year."

"Will that be my birthday gift?" We headed back to the van.

"I'll knit you an amazing scarf. You'll want to wear it all year round. Everyone will want a hand-knitted scarf from me."

"I can't wait."

I was unlocking the door when something hard was pressed against my back.

"Don't turn around. I have a gun. Get in and drive."

Chapter 16

"Holly, what's the matter?" Alice jiggled the handle of the van. "Oh! Who's that behind you?" She was still carrying Meatball, and he started to whine. He must be picking up on my panic as the gun dug into my back.

"Alice, run." My voice came out squeaky.

Her forehead wrinkled. "Run? What's going on?"

"Stay right where you are," the woman behind me said. "If you run, your friend dies."

Alice blinked rapidly. "What are you talking about? Who ... who are you? I'll have my security set on you. I ... oh, they don't know where I am."

I inwardly groaned.

"Get in the van and we can talk. You two in the front, I'll ride in the back. If anyone makes any sudden movements, I start shooting," the woman said.

Alice licked her lips. "We'd better do what she says. She looks very serious."

I held in a gasp. Alice had seen the woman's face. This gunslinger wouldn't let us go if she could be identified.

I unlocked the van with a shaking hand and slid into the seat.

Alice got in next to me, clutching Meatball to her chest. "Who is she? What does she want with us?"

"I have no clue. She didn't hand me a business card when she jabbed a gun in my back."

Alice's eyes filled with tears. "Is she kidnapping me? Do you think she knows who I am?"

"Less talking and more driving. Start the engine and head east." The woman settled behind us.

I started the engine, my foot shaking so badly it slid off the gas pedal several times. I reversed the van and headed away from the cat café. "What do you want with us? We don't have any money." I glanced at Alice. Maybe this was a kidnap and ransom attempt, but why had she shoved the gun in my back and not gone straight for Alice?

"I don't want your money," she said.

"You're not going to sell us into some terrible slave gang, are you?" Alice hugged Meatball.

"No! I'm not doing anything like that. I don't know anything about that." The woman's tone was agitated. "Just drive. I need to think."

I tried to still my racing heart as I snatched glimpses of the woman in the rearview mirror. "Emily, is that you?"

Alice gasped. "You're Emily Smithers? Of course. I see the similarities from the picture I've seen."

"Stop talking," the woman said.

"Oh! What a relief. You're not kidnapping me." Alice almost sounded happy. We were still stuck in a van with an angry woman and her gun.

"This isn't a kidnap attempt. Why would I kidnap you?" the woman said.

"Um, I don't know. Why would you?" Alice glanced at me. "I'm not important. But you, if you're Emily Smithers, you're very important."

The woman sitting behind me sighed. "I'm Emily. And I'm no one special. But I got a call that someone was asking questions about me. I had to come and check it out."

"Sophie called you! That's what she must have done when she went to check your contact details. And she seemed like such a nice lady." Alice shook her head.

"Sophie's a very nice woman. She always lets me know when someone comes around asking questions. She said you two were particularly nosy and wanted to know all about me."

"Do people often come to the café looking for you?" I said.

"Keep driving. We need to go somewhere quieter."

Alice's knees jiggled up and down. "Please, don't kill us. We're really very nice when you get to know us. I'll give you whatever you want if you let us go. I've got several tiaras I never use. You could have those, sell the stones, or wear them around the house. Whatever you like."

"Tiaras? What are you talking about?" Emily said.

"Alice, you shouldn't say anything else," I said. Campbell was going to kill me when he found out I'd gotten Alice into so much trouble. That was if Emily didn't kill us first.

"Hang on, I thought I recognized you." Emily shuffled over in the seat. "You're that princess from Audley Castle."

"Um, no. You're mistaken." Alice bit her bottom lip.

"You are! Why are you interested in me?" Emily's tone suggested her shock at discovering she'd kidnapped a princess.

"Because we really do need to speak with you," I said. "It's important."

"And who are you? Some duchess, I suppose?" Emily said.

"No! I'm Holly Holmes. I work in the castle kitchen."

"And she's my best friend, so please don't kill her. It'll take me ages to find another friend who can bake so well," Alice said.

"Alice," I grumbled under my breath.

Emily snorted. "Whatever you say, Princess. Take the next left and drive for three miles. You'll see a green signpost for Turnkey Woods. Drive to the end of the parking lot and stop."

I nodded, trying to calm my racing thoughts as we headed away from civilization and into the countryside. Emily was taking us to a secluded spot. That wouldn't be good for us. I briefly considered yanking the steering wheel to the side and running us off the road, but then we could all end up dead.

I turned along a dirt track that led to the parking lot. There were three other cars there, but there was no one around to disturb us.

"What happens now?" I said. "Are you going to walk us into the woods and get rid of us?"

"I need to know why you're looking for me," Emily said. "I don't know you. We didn't go to school together. Why did you lie to Sophie?"

"That's true. But I do know some of your old school friends, and they're in trouble," I said. "We're not here to cause you problems."

"Who are you talking about?"

"Jacob Marchwood. And I met some of his other friends. Adam, Bruce, Dexter. They were having a reunion party."

"I know about that. I got the invite."

"Why didn't you go? You can't live that far away," I said.

"I cut ties with that lot a while back. It was for the best."

I risked twisting in my seat. The look in Emily's eyes suggested she was more panicked than angry. "Do you really have a gun?"

She blinked several times and licked her lips. "I do. And I will use it."

"Is it a real gun?" I said.

Her bottom lip wobbled, and she reached into her purse.

Alice ducked and covered Meatball. "Look out!"

My heart thundered in my chest, but it slowed as Emily brought out a water pistol.

"I didn't stop to think what I was doing. I panicked. Sophie said there were two of you, and I didn't know why you were here. Now I've met you, I ... I don't think you're here to make trouble. Especially now I know who you are." Her gaze flicked to Alice.

"You abducted us with a water pistol!" Alice shook her head. "I'm never going to live this down. Don't you dare tell Rupert about this, Holly. He'll tease me forever."

"I needed to make sure you weren't working for someone else." Emily ducked her head. "I've never even held a real gun."

"Emily, is somebody after you? Is that why you're keeping a low profile?" I said.

"You wouldn't understand." She slumped back.

"I think I know more than you realize. Do you know what happened to Adam and Bruce?"

"Bruce!" She jerked upright. "I heard about Adam falling off the roof of Marchwood Manor. The papers reported it as an accident."

"The papers are wrong," I said. "There's evidence Adam was in a fight before he fell. The police are looking into it as a murder. And then Bruce was found the other night. It looked like a suspected drug overdose, but the evidence suggests otherwise. They were both killed."

Emily slumped forward and her breath came out shaky. "I had no idea about Bruce. What a stupid thing to do.

Everyone who knew him would have told you he'd never touch drugs. He hated them."

"Have you any idea who killed Adam and Bruce?" I said. "The fact they died so close together isn't a coincidence."

She lifted her head. The despair on her face made my heart ache. This woman was in serious need of help. "This is Bruce's fault. If only he hadn't been obsessed with recording everything, we wouldn't be in this mess."

"Did he film something when you went to the viral testing facility?" I said. "Is that what this tracks back to?"

She shifted in her seat. "You really don't want to be involved with this. Some secrets are meant to stay hidden."

"You're doing a good job of staying hidden," I said. "I'm not sure it's doing you any good, though."

"I was right to hide. Adam and Bruce's murders have proven that nowhere is safe. When Jacob contacted me and said he was getting the gang back together, I was horrified. I knew it would lead to trouble."

"What kind of trouble?" I said.

"The murder kind of trouble," Alice said.

Emily nodded. "As soon as I heard Jacob was dragging up the past, I arranged to take a year-long sabbatical. I planned to wipe the slate clean. Move away. See if I could start over. I was thinking another country, somewhere in Europe. Somewhere where no one knows me."

"Emily, are these deaths related to the conspiracy gang? Did you uncover something?" I asked.

"Was it aliens?" Alice whispered.

Emily gave a strangled laugh. "That dumb gang was supposed to be fun. We'd get together, hang out, and have a laugh. It was a way to blow off steam while we dreamed about moving away. Then everything went wrong." She dropped her head and began to cry.

"Are other people at risk?" I said.

"We're all at risk. Everyone who learns the truth is vulnerable."

"Is that why those people are trying to keep Holly out of this?" Alice said. "She's had visits from dubious types warning her to steer clear."

Emily lifted her head and wiped her cheeks. "Dubious types? What are you talking about?"

"I was out walking my dog and was approached by a guy in a black suit. He told me to stay away," I said.

"Oh! I don't know anything about that," Emily said.

"Then I was approached by a woman. She started out all friendly but then asked questions about the murder at Marchwood Manor. She also told me to stay away," I said.

"I scared her off," Alice said.

"You should both stay out of this," Emily said.

"It's too late for that," I said. "We have to get to the bottom of these murders. And if you and your friends are still at risk, we need to find out who's doing it quickly."

"You can't help! No one can. I wish I'd never joined that stupid gang. Once we left school and I went to college, I figured I could forget all about it, move on and enjoy life, but it was always lurking at the back of my mind. I always worried that it would return to haunt me."

"Emily, where were you four nights ago? It was the night of Jacob's party at Marchwood Manor," I said.

"It wasn't me who killed Adam or Bruce, if that's what you think. I wouldn't go anywhere near that party. But I don't have an alibi. I was home alone. Actually, I was checking flights to Malta. I've got some colleagues at a Maltese university. I thought I could do a couple of semesters there, then move around Europe, teaching now and again to keep my hand in."

"Why would you do that? Nothing bad happened to Adam until the end of the party. They were both still alive," I said.

"I was scared. Jacob was stirring up the past. I could see the problems that would cause. I decided to get away while I could. I sent a few emails, so there'll be records of those. That's all I can offer you. It wasn't me. I never wanted any of them to die."

"You should come back with us," Alice said. "See your old friends. Maybe they'll listen to you and be more careful. Or it could be a case of safety in numbers."

"I can't. I won't risk it. I stayed away because I needed to stay safe. I'm leaving the country before it's too late." Emily's gaze went to the door.

"Too late for what?" I said.

"Too late for me."

"Can't you tell us anything? Why does someone want you dead? What do you know that's worth killing for?" I said.

"The only advice I can give you is to trust no one." Emily's hand went to the door.

"Wait! What do you know about Simone Matthews?" I said.

"Simone?" Her expression grew panicked. "Is she ... dead?"

"Not that I know of, but she disappeared after Eleanor died. Have you heard from her since then?"

"I haven't. Now, leave me alone, before it's too late for both of you." Emily yanked open the door and dashed away through the trees.

I reached over and shut the door. I sat in my seat, my insides shaking.

"That was all rather serious," Alice said. "I don't know whether to laugh or cry."

"And I've got more questions than answers," I said. "She really thought we'd come to kill her. I'm glad you were here. Once she realized who you were, she dropped her guard."

"Maybe she was foolish to do so. After all, I'm sure you get assassin princesses. If not, perhaps I could be the first." The color returned to Alice's cheeks. "I could have found my calling. An assassin princess for hire. No job too bloody or too difficult."

"Don't suggest that to your parents, or they'll send you back to finishing school." I stared into the trees.

"What do we do now?" Alice said. "Emily was terrified. Scared enough to rip up her whole life and flee the country."

"Which, unfortunately, leads back to this government conspiracy idea. Maybe she's scared because there is some secret agency after her. She wouldn't be able to stop them. If it was just some old school friend with a grudge, the group could gang up on them, but this seems so much bigger."

"You're not giving up though, are you?" Alice said. "I feel like we're close. And we did find the knitting lead all on our own. Campbell would never have looked into that."

"We should try to find Simone. She was the first one in the gang to go missing. That could be important. She could have uncovered the secret, told the others, and then fled before things got serious."

Alice sighed. "We have a big problem if you plan to do that. How on earth do you find someone who doesn't want to be found?"

"Let's head back to the castle," I said. "I've got an idea."

Chapter 17

"Those banana and apricot muffins were amazing, Holly." Saracen looked up from the laptop he was working on and lifted his empty plate. "Have you got more samples to try?"

"I'm happy to keep feeding you, so long as you keep searching for information on the mysterious Simone Matthews." I opened the plastic box I'd brought with me and handed over a slice of coconut cream pie.

"Have you got any of that delicious chocolate mocha cake?" Alice peeked into the box. "I keep thinking about how yummy it is. I wish I could get away with eating it three times a day. The Cake Diet. That's a new idea."

"It's probably been done before. I haven't got any mocha cake, it's not suitable for Saracen's diet. A slice of that would mess with his diabetes."

He grunted and hunched his shoulders. It had taken Saracen a while to get used to his condition, but he was managing nicely, so long as I supplied him with tasty, doctor approved treats.

"What can you offer me?" Alice sat on the couch next to me, her feet tucked underneath her and Meatball snuggled on her lap.

I checked in the box and gave her a piece of pie.

After our encounter with Emily, we'd headed back to the castle. Rather than go straight to Campbell, who'd no doubt tear my head off when he learned about what happened, I'd enlisted Saracen's help. He was always willing to lend a hand, so long as I gave him tasty fuel while he worked.

He stared at the screen and tapped the table with his fingers. "Are you sure this woman isn't some sort of secret agent? There's not much to go on. No medical records, bank account, or online profiles. She definitely doesn't want people to know where she is."

"I'm willing to consider anything. These murders are such a puzzle," I said. "I was thinking this was a simple case of murder, but now, crazy conspiracy theory is looking likely."

"Something must link the two murders," Alice said. "My thinking is still aliens."

Saracen's brow wrinkled. He opened his mouth to speak, but I shook my head.

"We'll keep aliens off the table for now," I said.

Alice huffed and ate some pie.

"You reckon this Simone is your missing link in all this?" Saracen said.

"Not for certain," I said, "but she could be involved. She was a part of the conspiracy gang."

"And then you have that unfortunate girl who killed herself. That's very suspicious," Alice said.

"Who are we talking about?" Saracen asked.

"Eleanor Carrell. She died ten years ago. Simone ran off after it happened," I said.

"Supposedly to a university in America, which I don't believe," Alice said.

"Maybe she knew what Eleanor was going to do and felt guilty because she didn't stop her," I said. "Simone could have run away because she felt so bad."

"We'll have to find her and ask her to see if that's true," Alice said.

I blew out a breath. "We have Eleanor's suicide, Simone Matthews running off and no one hearing from her, Adam being pushed off Marchwood Manor, and Bruce murdered but his death made to look like a suicide."

"And the rest of the group are probably next," Alice said.

I groaned. "Don't say that. Although Dexter is struggling. He always seems drunk."

"Maybe he's an alcoholic. Drinking to hide from his guilt?" Alice said.

"He must be hiding from something," I said. "And whenever I talk to Jacob about the conspiracy gang, he makes out it was a bit of a laugh and a joke. Nothing serious."

"Which could also be a cover," Alice said. "He's using humor to divert attention from something more serious. He knows what really happened, but won't talk about it in case it makes him the next target."

"Well, whatever links them, it's something worth killing for," Saracen said.

Alice dabbed coconut cream off the side of her mouth. "We should still consider the alien angle. Everyone knows the government covers up our contact with aliens. They want everyone to believe we're the only intelligent life in this galaxy. That can't be possible. I was reading the other day that there are billions of planets out there. This can't be the only habitable one. Aliens are real."

"And they came to Appledore because it's a hotbed of political activity and they needed to make friends?" I said.

"They could have identified the viral testing place. They wanted to check it out and make sure it wasn't a threat,"

Alice said. "Aliens could be hiding in the woods and we wouldn't even know it."

"You need to give up on the alien theory," I said.

"No, I refuse to. It's an excellent theory. You'll be sorry when I uncover the truth and get to be the first to say hello to ET."

"I don't know about the little green men, Princess Alice," Saracen said. "But I have heard about the virus testing place."

"Have you ever been there?" I said.

"Nope. Never needed to."

"We should go," Alice said.

Saracen rubbed the back of his neck. "That place is off limits."

"Don't tell me you're scared of the aliens, Saracen," Alice said.

"You won't find any aliens there, Princess," he said. "But I've heard rumors about that place. All kinds of weird tests happened. It wasn't just viral weapons they were testing, they were using hallucinogenic drug trials on the enemy and our own soldiers, trying to turn them into lethal killing machines."

"Just like Campbell." Alice sounded breathless.

Saracen's eyebrows shot up. "Err, something like that."

"It makes sense why they wouldn't want anyone poking about, if that's what they were up to. There's no one working there now, is there?" I said.

"The place was shut down years ago," Saracen said. "I doubt there's even CCTV there."

"Then there's no harm in going to take a look," Alice said.

"What are you expecting to find?" I said. "If the site's been decommissioned, they'll have taken away any useful information."

"Someone always leaves something useful behind," Alice said. "You just need to know where to look."

From the petulant expression on her face, there was no way I'd talk her out of this. "If we're quick, we can take a look round tonight."

"I need to pass this by the boss," Saracen said, "especially if Princess Alice is coming with us."

"If you tell Campbell, we definitely won't be going," I said.

"We're going. That's an end to it," Alice said. "Holly, you always listen to your gut, and I'm doing the same with mine. It's telling me we'll find the answers at this place. We'll find our little green men. Although I bet they're not even that little. Why would aliens be little and green, anyway?"

I exchanged an exasperated look with Saracen.

"Give me five minutes. I'll get in touch with Campbell and see what he thinks." Saracen left the room, his cell phone against his ear.

Alice jabbed a finger in my ribs. "Anyone would think you didn't want to solve this mystery."

"I have a right to be cautious about digging into this. After all, I've had two mysterious people warn me off, and a gun pressed in my back."

"It was a water pistol!"

"It was still scary when I didn't know that."

"It was, but it only goes to show you must be close to finding out the truth if you've got people telling you to stay away."

"What are we supposed to stay away from? And what if I don't like the truth when I find it?" I said. "What if it gets us into trouble?"

"We have Saracen and Campbell to back us up," Alice said.

"You have them on your side. I'm alone. There's no beefy security to look out for me."

"You're forgetting that Campbell saved you from being squished by Adam when he plummeted to his death." Alice petted Meatball's head.

"I'm in the mood for alien hunting. The truth is out there."

I quietly hoped Campbell would say no to the idea of visiting the site. I was listening to my gut, and it was screaming at me that this was a dumb, dangerous idea.

Saracen returned to the room. "Campbell isn't happy."

"He's saying I can't go?" Alice lifted her chin and crossed her arms over her chest.

A smiled flicker across Saracen's face. "Once he heard you were involved, he said he'd join us, but only if we leave now."

"What are we waiting for? Let's move." Alice set Meatball on the floor. She stood and hurried to the door.

"We're waiting for Campbell, Princess. He's picking us up. He knows the route to the facility," Saracen said.

Alice peered out the window. "I don't see him."

"He'll be here soon," Saracen said.

I stepped closer to Saracen. "Was he raging because Alice wants to visit the site?"

"When I mentioned Princess Alice was involved, he just sighed and agreed to it. The guy sounds exhausted. He's been butting heads all day with that idiot over at Marchwood Manor, Lee. I don't think he could face another fight with the Princess. You know she can be a bit ... stubborn."

Alice stood by the door with Meatball, both of them looking excited, as if they were about to go out on a long walk in their favorite park.

"He has my sympathies," I said.

A few minutes later, a vehicle pulled up outside Saracen's apartment.

Alice pulled open the door. "Campbell's here. Everybody out."

We piled into the SUV, Meatball happy to sit on my lap.

Campbell glanced at me, anger simmering in his eyes. "You've got a lead at the testing facility?"

"Not really. We've been searching for Simone Matthews," I said.

"Then you're wasting your time." Campbell turned the vehicle around and headed to the main exit. "Or rather, you've been wasting Saracen's time."

"I don't mind helping, boss," Saracen said. "I'm off duty."

"We're never off duty," Campbell said.

"Don't be angry with Saracen. We bribed him into helping us," I said.

"I guessed that. I can see the crumbs on his chest," Campbell said.

Saracen brushed a hand down his front. "Sorry, boss. I can never resist Holly's treats. I thought I was helping out, looking into one of the missing suspects in these murder investigations."

"Did you find anything useful about Simone?" Campbell said.

"She's a ghost," Saracen said. "I was thinking she's former covert ops. She knows how to make herself invisible online."

"When I looked into her, I hit a brick wall, too." Campbell headed west, toward Appledore. "I don't think she's relevant to these murders, though. She's been in the wind for a decade."

"We wondered if she had something to do with what happened to Eleanor Carrell," I said. "It's strange that she dies and then Simone vanishes."

"She didn't vanish though, did she," Campbell said. "Simone moved abroad. She kept in touch with her mom, although the contact wasn't frequent."

I sat back in my seat, twisting the strange threads of this mystery together and then pulling them apart. Was Simone the link that bound the group?

Campbell drove for fifteen minutes until we reached Appledore village. It was a similar size to Audley St. Mary but didn't come with its own grand castle.

We drove along increasingly narrow lanes, which became muddy and uneven.

Campbell came to a stop by a long metal gate. "We'll have to walk the rest of the way."

"Oh, I didn't think we'd be walking anywhere." Alice looked down at her pink kitten heels. "I don't have suitable footwear."

"There are boots in the back," Campbell said. "There'll be something in there to fit you."

"You want me to wear somebody else's boots?" Alice's nose wrinkled.

Campbell sighed and muttered something I didn't catch.

I leaned closer to Alice. "You were the one who wanted to do this."

She huffed out a breath. "The last person who wore the boots could have a foot infection or something gross. I don't want to catch anything nasty."

"Do you want to investigate this site to see if there are aliens here, or worry about a verruca?" I said.

She gave a dramatic sigh. "I suppose I can sacrifice my feet in the hunt for aliens. Help me find a suitable pair."

We climbed out the vehicle and headed around the back.

Campbell had the trunk open. He pulled out a pair of black boots. "These are probably closest to your size."

"Holly, inspect them." She waved a hand at me.

"What for?"

"Cleanliness. Spiders. Left behind foot fungus," she said.

"And if I find any of those gross things?" I shone my cell torch into the murky depths of the boots, then gave them to Meatball to sniff.

"Deal with them." She perched on the edge of the trunk, took off one of her pink kitten heels, and passed it to me. "Is there anything in them?"

"They look almost new." I handed her a boot and curtseyed.

She gingerly slid her foot into the boot. "These will do."

"I don't like to hurry you, Princess, but the light's fading. If you want to get a look round the site, we need to hurry," Campbell said.

She handed me her other shoe and slid on the next boot. "I'm ready. Let's go."

Campbell took the lead, with Saracen at the back. The path was narrow, so I had to stay behind Alice with Meatball. He was delighted to explore a new place. I had to keep encouraging him to move along because there were so many exciting scents to investigate.

"What's this?" Alice stopped by a large tree trunk.

"Keep out." I read the wonky sign nailed to the trunk. "That's encouraging."

"When the site was active, they had all kinds of signs up to discourage locals from being too interested in what was going on," Campbell said. "It doesn't matter now. The place is empty."

"You don't know that for sure," Alice said. "They could have left a few aliens behind."

Campbell did more muffled grumbling.

We walked a little farther and came to some barbed wire stretched over the path.

"That's not safe," Alice said. "Someone could cut themselves if they didn't see it."

"It's just another deterrent." Campbell pulled out wire cutters from his pocket and made short work of removing the barbed wire. "It's a dumb place to put it, though. You must get walkers around here."

"Oh! There's another sign." Alice hurried past Campbell. "Trespassers will be prosecuted. That doesn't apply to us."

"Are you really sure you want to look around?" Campbell said.

"You'll keep us safe," Alice said. "We can't get in any trouble when you're here."

"Don't be so sure about that," I said quietly.

"I heard that, Holmes," Campbell said.

"I see a fence up ahead." Alice bustled away.

"Princess Alice! Stay with us. We can't get separated." Campbell raced after her.

"Princess Alice seems convinced about the alien theory." Saracen walked along beside me.

"She's got a big imagination," I said.

"Don't you believe in aliens, Holly?"

"I've never met one."

"That you know of."

I chuckled. "You're telling me you believe in them?"

"I've seen strange things in my line of work."

"But not aliens." I looked up, surprised by his serious expression. "Saracen, don't fool around. You've seen aliens?"

"I didn't say that, but I have seen something that got me wondering."

"What was it?"

"I spent eight months on an operation trying to identify strange lights in the sky. It was around the time when the war on terror got started. Everyone was on high alert. People were convinced we were days away from an attack. I was assigned to a unit whose task was to figure out where the lights were coming from, and if they were a threat or signal."

"What did you find?"

"That's the weird thing. We mapped every possible source the light could have come from. We looked at the ground sources, aerial sources, you name it, we looked at it and tested it to see how the lights were being generated. We came up blank. We had some top experts working alongside us, and we got nothing. Then one day, they stopped."

"You think it was a signal from another planet or a spaceship?"

"I'm not saying either of those things, but weird stuff goes on in this world. You've been up the east turret steps plenty of times to know there are some things you can't explain."

I shuddered at the thought of the east turret. It was always cold, a little spooky, and I never liked to hang around it for long. "If an alien jumps out, I'm hiding behind you."

Saracen grinned. "That's what I'm paid for. Protector of princesses and slayer of aliens."

"Holly, come see this," Alice called from up ahead.

I rounded the corner to find her standing by a twelve-foot fence with barbed wire at the top. "This must be the boundary of the testing facility."

"And clever Campbell has found us a way in. It'll mean sliding under the fence, though. I should have worn something more practical for this mission." Alice looked down at her pale pink silk gown.

"We can always turn back," I said. "Come back another day when you're suitably dressed."

"Absolutely not. We've come this far. I'm not aborting the mission because I'm not dressed like James Bond. Campbell, you go first, show us how it's done."

"I'll cut the wire some more. It'll make it easier to get through." Campbell made a large enough hole so we could duck through without getting too muddy.

Once inside, I looked around. The place had an eerie quiet to it. It was like the wildlife was staying away. "These viral weapons, there wouldn't still be any here?"

"Definitely not," Campbell said. "The only stuff that may be left behind is old bits of furniture. All government agencies have to decommission sites before they leave."

"So they don't leave incriminating evidence behind," Alice said. "I know all about that. I've seen the movies."

"We've got half an hour before we need to turn back," Campbell said.

"We can't cover the whole site in half an hour," Alice said.

"It would help narrow things down if we knew what to look for," Campbell said.

"You should know that better than we do," I said. "You're the one interested in this conspiracy link."

"It has legs," he said.

"I've got an idea," Alice said. "It'll help to narrow down our options. We need to put ourselves in the heads of teenagers. You're a bored teenager, looking for fun with your friends. You find this place, sneak in, then what do you do?" She turned in a slow circle.

"You need to find somewhere out of sight," I said. "If this place was still active when they were looking round, they wouldn't want anyone to spot them while they drank and fooled around."

"They wouldn't have been able to get inside the main building, there would have been guards. And to get in, you'd have needed a swipe card or an access code," Saracen said.

"Depending on what they were testing here, there may have been fingerprint pass codes and retinal scans, too,"

Campbell said.

"So, we wouldn't try to go inside the main building. What about those storage sheds over there?" Alice pointed to a row of six sheds.

"Let's start there," I said. "See if there's anything useful."

We headed to the first storage shed. It was empty. The second one was the same.

Alice tutted and hurried to the third shed. She pulled it open and yelped, flinging herself back and bumping into Campbell as a pigeon shot out the door.

She laughed as she righted herself and brushed down her dress. "Silly me, being startled by a bird. I didn't hurt you, did I, Campbell?"

"I'm fine, Princess. Let me go in first, though. You never know what you could stumble across."

"Just so long as it's not aliens, I don't mind," I said.

Alice poked her tongue out at me. "I think the alien theory is as valid as anything you could come up with."

I decided not to test that as I searched around the third storage shed. Apart from a couple of old rusty buckets and an empty filing cabinet that had been tipped on its side, there was nothing.

The fourth and fifth shed were the same. The final shed had a metal bar over the double doors.

Campbell eased the bar off and slid the door open. He stared into the gloom. "It looks like they didn't clear everything out of here."

"Let me see." Alice peered around his shoulder. "There are crates inside. This is what we've been looking for."

"Alice, they're probably empty," I said. "Don't get your hopes up that you'll find anything exciting hiding in those trunks. There are no alien autopsies in here."

"It does no harm to look. Hurry up, all of you."

Campbell muttered something that sounded quite rude under his breath. Saracen chuckled and strolled in behind Alice.

I nudged Campbell with my elbow as I passed him. "Just remember, you signed up for this job."

"Sometimes, protecting a princess is harder than doing a tour of duty in war-torn Serbia."

"We'll take a quick look inside the boxes, then get out of here. Once Alice's curiosity has been sated, she'll lose interest in this place."

"Maybe she shouldn't." He walked alongside me into the shed.

"Do you still think there's a connection to what the group found here and Adam and Bruce's murders?"

"I do. I've been following a lead I got out of Lee. It's about a drug they were testing at this place."

"It had bad side effects? Did they try to cover it up?"

"No, it has to do with—"

The door slamming shut behind us had me jumping.

Meatball barked and raced to the door.

I whirled around, my stomach dropping as the metal bar slid into place.

Campbell charged to the door and tried to open it. It didn't budge. He slammed his shoulder against it.

Alice dashed to my side. "Holly, what's going on?"

I grabbed her hand, my heart racing. "Someone just locked us in."

Chapter 18

"We're trapped!" Alice gave a little sob. "Campbell, get us out of here."

"I'm working on it, Princess." He charged the door again.

"That was a metal bar keeping the door shut. You won't bust through that easily," I said, grabbing Meatball. He was pawing at the door and whining.

Campbell grunted. "Just you watch. Saracen, I could do with some help."

"On it, boss." Saracen joined Campbell by the door.

"If we hit it together, the hinges could be rusty. The door is only made of wood," Campbell said.

Alice clutched my arm as they charged the door with their shoulders. "Who'd want to lock us in here?"

"Someone determined to ensure we don't discover the truth behind the murders," I said.

"Do you think they followed us here?"

I winced as Campbell and Saracen charged the door again. "Or they were watching the site, making sure no one turned up to look round."

"I didn't see anyone else here," Alice said.

"It's breaking," Campbell said. "One more time should do it."

"He's so incredible," Alice said. "Campbell is such a hero."

"He'd have been more heroic if he convinced you not to come here in the first place," I said.

"Aren't you glad we did? Getting locked in here simply proves a point. There are secrets about this place. Secrets that people want to remain hidden. And we're not going to let that happen. We will find those aliens."

There was a splintering of wood as Campbell and Saracen burst through the door.

"You're so clever." Alice raced over, her arms wide as if she meant to hug Campbell. At the last second she stopped herself and her cheeks glowed bright pink. "Good work, Campbell. I knew you'd get us out of this mess. You too, Saracen."

"Saracen, you stay here with Princess Alice and Holly. I'll see if the idiot who locked as in was dumb enough to stick around." Campbell shot off into the gloom.

I set Meatball down and spent the next few minutes with Alice, opening empty crates and peering inside. After all the excitement of being locked in, it was all rather deflating. There were no clues, no alien artifacts, or anything helpful in the crates.

Campbell returned, a sour expression on his face. "Whoever locked us in is long gone. There are tire marks in the dirt. Someone used a bike to get here."

"Well, the secret they're keeping hidden isn't in these wooden crates," Alice said.

"Let's get you back to the castle, Princess," Campbell said. "That's enough excitement for one night."

"You're right. We can start searching again first thing tomorrow," Alice said.

Campbell's lips pressed together, and he shot me a glare.

"Haven't you got an afternoon tea with some friends in Cambridge tomorrow?" I said.

"Oh! I'd forgotten about that. I can cancel. They'll understand. This is much more important," Alice said.

"No, you should go," I said. "If we are being watched, you don't want anyone to get suspicious if we change our routines."

Alice bit her bottom lip. "I hadn't thought about that. You don't think they'll come after me, do you?"

"No! I absolutely don't," Campbell said. "Holly, stop scaring Princess Alice."

I glowered at him. I was trying to help. He'd wanted her out of danger. What was safer than having cream tea with a bunch of posh friends in a café in a crowded city?

"Maybe Holly's right. I did want to catch up with Tia and see if she's made progress with getting her boyfriend to propose. Don't do anything exciting without me, though. I don't want to miss out."

"I'll be at work," I said. "All I'll be doing is baking cakes and being yelled at by Chef Heston."

"And the Duke and Duchess have requested an escort to London," Campbell said. "I'll be taking a small team down there."

"We can't ignore these murders," Alice said. "Someone has to keep looking into them. Saracen, you do something useful while we're busy."

Saracen's eyebrows shot up. "Of course, Princess. I'll keep looking into Simone. I may be able to dig up something useful."

"Well, I suppose that's something. Let's go. I'm getting cold feet out here and I can't feel the end of my nose."

Campbell escorted Alice away from the broken door.

I was walking alongside Saracen, back to the SUV, when Meatball whined and dug at something on the ground.

I turned back to him. "You be careful. There'll be splinters around here. You don't want to get one of those in your paw."

He whined again and tugged at something with his teeth. I backtracked and joined him.

Saracen turned and looked back. "You coming, Holly?"

"I'll just be a second. I need to grab Meatball." I scooped him up.

He was holding a ragged piece of paper in his mouth.

"What have you got there?" I eased it out of his teeth and flattened it out. My heart raced into my throat as I read the message.

If you want to know the truth, come here alone tomorrow night at seven.

It was signed off with the letter *S*.

I blinked several times, not believing what I was seeing. An S. Was this from Simone Matthews? Had she left me a note? Was she in Appledore? Why had she come back after all this time?

"Good boy, Meatball. I wouldn't have seen that if you hadn't dug it out for me."

He licked my cheek and settled his paws over my arm, happy to be carried back to the vehicle.

Saracen looked over his shoulder and raised a hand when he saw me following him.

I signaled back I was fine, but I was anything but fine. Was this note really from Simone, or was it an attempt at subterfuge by the people warning me off? Did they want me to come back tomorrow night on my own and silence me for good?

As hard as I tried, I couldn't believe this was some big government cover-up. And I didn't believe Alice and her alien ideas. I didn't even believe Campbell.

"What do you think, Meatball? We need to find out what's going on. Something bad happened here."

He licked my cheek again. "Woof, woof."

"I agree. I need to do this. Two people have been killed, and more could die. It's time to find out what's going on. And this time, I won't be involving the family."

⁕⁕⁕

"I'm not sure about you doing this." Gran followed me around the apartment as I grabbed my boots and pulled on my jacket the next evening.

Although I'd kept the note a secret from Alice and Campbell, I'd shared what I'd found with her. "I'll have Meatball to protect me. He's great at sensing danger."

"As sturdy as he is, Meatball can't protect you from a ninja secret agent intent on destroying you. Don't go, Holly."

"Gran, I have to. And you know where I'll be. If I'm not back in an hour, get in touch with Campbell and tell him what's going on."

"That's not good enough. I should come with you."

"No! I don't want anyone else involved in this mystery. I was lucky Campbell didn't knock me out after I involved Princess Alice."

"Then I insist you text me every ten minutes with updates," Gran said. "And take pictures. Take a picture of this woman you're meeting, so I know who she is. If anything bad happens to you, I can give the information to the police and they can hunt her down. That's if I don't get to her first."

I kissed her cheek. "Gran, everything will be okay. I'm not sure what's going on with Simone Matthews, but she's scared about something. If I bring anyone else with me or alert the police or castle security, it could scare her off. I have to talk to her. I think she knows something about these murders."

"Maybe she knows about them because she did them," Gran said. "I bet you haven't thought about that."

I'd thought about all kinds of things last night as I'd tried to sleep. "I promise, I'll text you to keep you up-to-date with what's going on. Now, I have to go. I'm meeting her in half an hour."

"Take this." She thrust a can of pepper spray in my hand. "Keep it close. Use it."

After several more hugs from Gran, I hurried out the door with Meatball, grabbed the keys to one of the work's vans, and we made the journey back to Appledore.

Several times I slowed, indecision wavering through me. I shouldn't do this alone. But the note had been clear. And I really wanted to know the truth. Who killed Adam? Why had Bruce's death been made to look like suicide? Then there was the mystery of Eleanor Carrell's suicide all those years ago. I had to get to the bottom of this.

"You're my lookout, Meatball," I said. "If anything seems suspicious, you bark as loudly as you can. Lots of growling and plenty of hackles raised. We have to look like we mean business."

"Woof, woof!" He wagged his tail, looking like the least intimidating dog I'd ever met. But Meatball had a fierce bark and always picked up my emotions when I was worried. I could rely on him if there was trouble.

I parked at the same gate Campbell had driven us to yesterday and climbed out. I had a head torch on, a hand torch, and my cell phone. I also had the pepper spray in my pocket.

I hurried along the path, my gaze shifting from side to side, looking out for anyone lurking in the shadows.

Meatball stuck close to me, not distracted by the alluring scents surrounding him. We were on a mission, and he knew not to get distracted.

I climbed through the hole Campbell had made in the fence and made my way to the sheds. I checked my watch. I was right on time.

I looked around, but the place was silent and still.

"Have you come alone?"

My shoulders tensed and my stomach flip-flopped at the sound of a quiet woman's voice behind me. "It's just me and my dog. Is it okay to turn around and see you?"

There was a soft sigh. "It's fine. I'm too tired to keep on hiding."

I turned and came face-to-face with a haggard-looking Simone Matthews. She was thin, her hair cut close to her face. There were dark circles under her eyes. I discreetly snapped a picture on my phone and hoped I hadn't just taken a shot of my palm. I'd send it to Gran when I got a second.

"I don't know who you are, but it seems you won't stop poking around," she said.

"I'm Holly Holmes. I work at Audley Castle. And you're Simone Matthews."

"That's right. So, Holly Holmes, why are you so interested in what went on here ten years ago?"

"Ten years ago? You mean Eleanor's suicide?"

She scrubbed a hand down her face. "That's right. I've been haunted by that night ever since it happened."

"You've been gone a long time," I said. "People are worried about you."

"I kept in touch with those I cared about, but I needed to get away. I had a lot to think about. And I didn't want to draw attention to myself."

"Then you came back, and Adam and Bruce died. Simone, did you come back to kill them?"

She slumped against the shed, her head down. "I couldn't believe it when I heard."

"Where were you when you found out they were dead?"

Her tired gaze met mine. "Answer me one question first, why are you so interested?"

"Because I was there when Adam was killed. I was standing directly underneath him. He almost landed on me. It shook me up. I needed to make sure it was just an accident. Then Bruce died, and I realized something was wrong. I had to find out what was going on."

She tilted her head. "Most people would have put it down to tragedy, or bad luck affecting an old group of friends. Not you."

"I've been called nosy a few times," I said. "And something was telling me things were very wrong here. I hate to see an injustice done."

Simone's gaze moved to the main building, but I wasn't certain she was looking at anything. Her gaze was haunted, an old pain shining in her eyes.

"I was three hundred miles away when I heard about Adam. Just like you, I knew it wasn't an accident. The past can only stay hidden for so long."

"And is that past connected to this place?" I said. "You said in your note that you'd tell me the truth about what went on."

"Just you." Her gaze narrowed and flicked back to me. "I saw you with those guys last night."

"Oh! I don't work for them. I'm a baker."

She huffed out a laugh. "Whatever. I've met security guys like that before. They react first and ask questions later. I didn't trust them not to arrest me if I showed myself."

"You trust me?"

She glanced at me. "I'm not sure I trust anyone."

"I'm not here to judge. We all make mistakes."

"I doubt you've ever killed anyone."

I swallowed. "Have you?"

"As good as. I've been holding onto this for so long that I've almost forgotten how to live. This guilt has been eating away inside me. When I let it go, I'm not sure what will be left, or if I'll like the woman I've become. I don't think much of her now."

"What have you got to be guilty about?"

She dropped her head down. "You'll hate me if I tell you."

"Did you and your friends see something bad at this facility? It got you in trouble?"

"Trouble definitely found us after that night," Simone said.

"What did you see?" I said.

"Do you know about this place?" She nodded at the abandoned building.

"I've heard different rumors about it. It used to test food products?"

"No, it definitely didn't do that. Try again."

I took a shallow breath. "Viral weapons for use in warfare?"

"Possibly. When my friends and I came here, security was tight. We were interested in it. We were sure something dodgy was going on."

"Did you find out what that something dodgy was?" I said. "Is it something that killed your friends?"

"Walk with me, Holly." Simone pushed away from the building. "I'll give you a tour. Show you around. I have a lot to tell you. Since you refuse to stop poking around in my past, you deserve to know everything."

I gulped and looked down at Meatball.

His tail was wagging, and he seemed relaxed. He wasn't picking up bad vibes from Simone. And although she was tense, neither was I. If anything, she seemed beaten, as if she'd given up trying to run from whatever was haunting her.

"Okay, why don't you tell me the truth?"

Chapter 19

"I need to take you back ten years." Simone walked toward the main building. "I was seventeen, excited about the future, trying to figure out which college to go to, and dealing with a serious crush I had on Adam Remus. The typical teenage stuff, really."

I walked along beside her, my senses on high alert. "Back to when Eleanor was still alive?"

She glanced at me and nodded. "How did you hear about what happened to Eleanor?"

"I met her dad at the party Jacob held at Marchwood Manor. I put my foot in it when I asked about her."

"I feel so sorry for Mr. Carrell. That should never have happened to Eleanor."

"Happened? I thought she committed suicide."

"It's complicated." Simone stopped outside a set of double doors. "Do you want to take a look inside?"

"Is it safe?"

"There's no one here, so we can't get in trouble. It was different when we were here as teenagers."

"Lead the way."

"We'll have to go round the side," Simone said. "I've been here a couple of times since I came back to

Appledore, so I know a way in. Even though I should have stayed away, I keep getting drawn back."

"If you were in the area, why didn't you go to Jacob's reunion party?"

"Some reunion that was. Adam and Bruce are dead. Jacob should have known it was a stupid idea to revive the past."

"Are you worried you could be next?"

Simone tugged at a stiff door before it flew open. "Of course. That's why I dropped off the radar." She stepped inside a dark corridor, pulled out a torch, and flicked it on. "This is where it went wrong for us. You know what teenagers are like, we think we're invincible. The rules don't apply, and we can do anything we like and get away with it."

"Simone, what happened the night you came here with Eleanor? Did you see something you shouldn't?"

"We did, but it's probably not what you think."

"I have a friend who thinks this place has something to do with an alien conspiracy. Please tell me it wasn't little green men you discovered."

Simone chuckled softly. "No, it was nothing like that. Although I did wonder about this place. I was super into my conspiracy theories back then. I'd have loved it if it had been aliens."

"If not alien, then what?"

She looked around the damp, empty corridor. "This place tested drugs to be used against a foreign enemy."

"My viral weapons idea was close?" Campbell had been about to tell me something to do with drug tests at this place. Was this what he meant?

"Close enough. They probably did that here, too. It was a secure place. Guards, wire fencing, guns. It was almost impossible to get into."

"But you did get in," I said. "You uncovered something that should have remained a secret. Is that why the government is after you?"

"I'm surprised you know so much and are still alive," Simone said.

"I'm glad I am."

"Don't count on that staying the same for long."

"That sounds like a threat." I looked at the door. I could still get out.

"No, not from me. I'm not going to hurt you. I'm glad to have someone to talk to. Keeping silent about something so dark is painful."

"What are you keeping quiet about?"

Simone was quiet for a moment. "The thing with these government agencies is they tread close to the line of what's legal. When it comes to winning wars, they often cross that line. This place had some weird stuff going on. We must have come here a dozen times and spent hours sitting on the other side of the fence and watching the guards."

"What did they do?"

"Nothing exciting. But trucks came in and out. And there were loads of science nerds around. A few soldiers, too. We began to notice a pattern. The guards would change over at the same time every evening. Sometimes, they didn't get it right. They got lazy, or bored, I don't know. There were a few minutes when the place wasn't guarded."

"And you snuck in?"

"We didn't all go in. Only one of us." She pulled a cell phone from her back pocket, opened a video, pressed play, and handed it to me.

I squinted at the blurry, shaking image. I recognized the building we were standing in and saw some guys walking around in uniforms.

"Eleanor! Stop her!"

"That was Adam," Simone said.

A person streaked past the camera, her hair flying out behind her. Whoever was holding the camera followed her movement. I recognized Eleanor from the picture I'd seen of them in Marchwood Manor.

"She's out of control." That voice on the recording was Simone.

Several other people raced past in a blur.

"She's going inside. Don't let her get away. They'll know what we did." That was Adam again.

"Wait! Eleanor! Don't go that way," Simone yelled.

There was a scream and several cries of alarm.

"I think … she's dead." Adam's tone was shaky.

Then the video cut off.

I looked up at Simone, ice sliding through my veins. "Eleanor didn't kill herself?"

Simone licked her lips and looked away. "You can probably guess who was filming that night."

"Bruce. When I met him, he had a camera around his neck and was talking about always keeping recordings."

"That was on one of his old camcorders he used that night. He made a copy of the recording and sent it to me a while back. I couldn't believe he'd kept it. After all these years. Why keep something so dark?"

"What was wrong with Eleanor? She looked terrified. Was she being chased?"

Simone tipped her head back. "I liked Eleanor, but she got on my nerves. She was such a goody two shoes. She was always focused on her studies and the future."

"Plus, you had a crush on Adam, the guy she was dating."

"Yeah, that definitely didn't help me warm to her."

"Did you do something to her that night?" I said.

"I didn't do anything, other than keep my mouth shut for too long." Simone paced the corridor. "She used to date Adam, but he was getting really intense and pushy. He wanted to take the next step with her, but she wasn't ready. She was thinking of finishing things with him."

"I thought he left her?"

"No, that's the story we told everyone. Eleanor had talked to a couple of us about it, and I decided to mention it to Adam. It was a bitchy thing to do, and I regret it. He took the news badly. He said she couldn't break it off with him. Adam had an ego. He was one of the most popular guys in school. No one dumped him."

"But Eleanor wanted something different?"

"She wanted a future without Adam in it. So, she ended things. He was raging mad that night. He said he wanted to teach her a lesson."

"What did he do to her?"

"He wanted her to loosen up, change her mind, and get back with him. We all went out together that night. He asked her several times to get back together and things got tense. Eleanor took a walk and Adam started drinking a lot."

"Were you all there when she died? Could you have saved her? Is that the secret?" I said.

"We were. But I doubt there was anything anyone could have done. We didn't even know what she was on."

"She'd taken drugs? Her death was from an overdose."

"Not knowingly." Simone pinched the bridge of her nose. "It was Adam's idea. And we encouraged him to do it. We thought it would be funny. You see, we knew the guard changeover pattern. So, we dared Adam to sneak into the testing lab and steal something when there was a gap in the security."

"He stole something from the lab and gave it to Eleanor?"

Simone nodded. "I never for a second expected him to get inside. Well, I thought he'd get past the gate but be spotted by a guard and have to make a run for it. I couldn't believe it when he made it all the way to the door. And then it wasn't locked. The last person who'd gone in hadn't shut it properly. He was in and out in five minutes. He was so full of himself when he came back. And he had this small packet of pills and a file of paperwork with him."

"You had no idea what he gave to Eleanor?"

"We were all drinking, all full of ourselves because one of us had broken into this top-secret place. He reckoned he'd seen some information about the pills when he'd grabbed them. He said it was pure LSD. He reckoned it would give us all an amazing high. Of course, I wasn't stupid enough to take it. No one else did. But he slipped a pill into Eleanor's drink."

My mouth fell open. "It could have been anything."

"I know! To begin with, she was fine. She seemed happy and was dancing around. She kept hugging Adam and saying she loved him. He looked so smug, like he'd won a prize. All he'd done was drug his girlfriend with heaven knows what. It got out of control so quickly. One minute, Eleanor was laughing and having a great time, then she said she felt hot. She started tugging at her clothes and saying she needed to cool down. We didn't know what to do. Then she got manic, then angry, then she ran off."

"And Bruce was recording all of this?"

"Not all of it. He sometimes took pictures instead of recordings. But he picked up his camcorder when Eleanor started saying she wasn't feeling great. You've seen the footage. She ran straight into the testing facility. We'd made a gap in the fence that we could get through. She raced inside and ran to the building. She was crying and screaming."

"And the guards caught her?"

"Almost. They saw her and started yelling, warning her to stay away. I panicked. They had guns, but I didn't think they'd shoot her. After all, she was just a drunk teenage girl."

"They didn't kill her, did they?"

"No, at the last second, Eleanor changed direction. She ran out of the facility and headed toward this huge drop. We all knew to be careful in these woods. If you go along the wrong path, it suddenly stops and there's a sheer rock face you can fall down."

Horror clutched at my heart. "Eleanor didn't stop?"

"That's right." Simone swallowed loudly and looked at the floor.

"What aren't you telling me? That's not the end of the story."

"We tried to get away, but the guards stopped us."

"They figured out what you'd done?" I asked.

"Only because Adam freaked out. He admitted to everything. He told the guards he broke in, stole the pills, and gave one to Eleanor. We were terrified. We figured we could go to jail. The guards talked for a couple of minutes, then called their supervisor. Some tough guy in a black suit came out, along with his blonde assistant."

A black suit and a blonde assistant? Could they be the people warning me off?

"None of you were arrested or charged with anything," I said. "When the case was investigated, we didn't find information about criminal records relating to this."

"Yeah, that's why I went into hiding. You see, what they tested in the lab wasn't strictly legal. Or rather, the fact they were testing drugs on human subjects before they passed clinical trials was a big problem."

"How do you know that?"

"From the file Adam stole. We didn't have a clue what the information in there was about, but the supervisor saw it and panicked. He made a deal with us."

"He kept your secret about Eleanor if you kept the secret about what the lab was really doing?"

"You got it." Simone's head dipped. "We made it look like she'd taken some drugs and thrown herself over the edge of the drop. The supervisor told the guards they'd seen nothing and told us never to come back."

"He didn't know Bruce had recorded the whole thing?"

"No. Bruce didn't miss any of it. He recorded when Eleanor lost control, took pictures of her body, and had an audio recording of the supervisor hushing us up."

"And that information has come out, hasn't it?" I said. "Is that why people are dying? You think word has gotten back to the government agency who hushed this up and now they're silencing you?"

Simone nodded. "They're killing off the conspiracy gang because they know we've got evidence that they were involved in this cover-up. They knew Eleanor's death wasn't a suicide. They prioritized their work over the death of a teenage girl."

"Have you been threatened recently? Is someone after you?"

"I feel like I'm being watched. I have ever since Eleanor died. Just after it happened, there was this guy hanging out at the school watching us. Then I saw him at my house. I was about ready to go traveling, so I pushed my plans forward, grabbed a cheap ticket abroad, and left."

"There was no university place in America?"

"No, I never went. I lied to my mom so she wouldn't worry about me vanishing. I've worked in dead-end jobs, usually cash in hand, always on the move. I didn't want my past to find me. It was stupid coming back here, but I

K.E. O'CONNOR

couldn't stay away, not after what happened to Adam and Bruce."

"You can only run from the past for so long. It catches up with you in the end."

"Maybe this is just my time. And I'm tired of hiding."

"Simone, you've lived with this horrible secret for a long time. If you go to the police and tell them what happened, they'll protect you."

"The local police are no good," she said. "They can't protect me from a covert government operation that wants to keep me quiet."

"Maybe they can't, but we've got great security at Audley Castle. They'll look after you."

"I don't care anymore. I want them to find me. I deserve it. Eleanor died a horrible death. She was terrified and confused. She had no idea what was happening to her. Adam should never have given her those drugs, but I should never have told him to do it. And when he suggested he teach Eleanor a lesson, I should have told him he was being a jerk and to leave her alone. I didn't. She irritated me, and I was jealous of her. I never thought what we did that night would end up with her dead and me on the run."

A scuffling noise outside the door made us both jump.

"They must have found me." Simone backed away along the corridor.

"Don't leave," I said. "Come with me. I've got someone who can help you."

"I'm beyond saving," Simone said. "The truth is going to come out soon, anyway."

"Stay and face it. Don't do this on your own."

The scuffling intensified and there was a scratching at the door as if someone was testing the lock.

"I have to go. I'm not ready for this."

"Do you know how the recording got out?" I hurried after Simone as she raced from door to door, trying to find an escape route.

"It was probably Bruce. He sent it to me ages ago. And I heard he'd been struggling. He could have given it to the others, or put it online on a conspiracy site. I have no idea. All I know is that the information is out there. And that means we're all dead."

"You said you were tired. You said you wanted to stop running. It looks like you're still running, though."

Simone found a door that opened. She checked inside the room. "It's all I know how to do. Holly, now you know the truth, you should consider disappearing too. Whichever government agency covered this up, they know you're looking into this. They're ruthless. They don't care what they need to do to keep their secrets safe. You know about Eleanor now, and you've seen what they've done to Adam and Bruce. You seem like a nice lady, even though you're too curious for your own good. I'd hate for you to be next."

I glanced around, paranoia traveling up my spine like a painful itch. "They won't come after me. I'm a nobody. I make cakes for a living."

"You also know too much. My advice, get out of here while you can." She dodged through the door and slammed it in my face.

There was a thump against the outside door.

I tensed before turning to it slowly. Was this the secret agency coming to get me?

Meatball growled as he approached the door.

With my heart thundering in my chest, I followed him. "Careful, Meatball. Let's hope we're not too late to make our escape."

Chapter 20

I inched toward the door, Meatball a pace in front of me, his hackles raised. "We can handle this. I'll open the door and we run. Whoever it is, I'll push them as hard as I can."

Meatball growled again, as if agreeing with me.

"We can do this. We just need to get back to the van and we'll be safe." My heart pounded so hard I felt dizzy, but I was determined this case wouldn't beat me. If it was some government snoop trying to silence me, he'd listen to reason. He wouldn't kill a defenseless woman and her dog.

But someone had killed Adam and Bruce. Was Simone right? Were these murders linked back to that terrible night ten years ago when a bunch of teenagers made a horrible mistake?

"Are you ready?" I whispered to Meatball.

His tail lowered, and he hunkered down as if about to pounce.

I grabbed an old piece of wood leaning up against the wall and held it in one hand. I reached for the door handle.

The scratching noises stopped.

I swallowed to dislodge the lump in my throat. Maybe, whoever it was, they were reaching for a gun. They were waiting on the other side of the door for me to come out.

I ducked low to make myself a smaller target, moved into a sprinter's stance, and barged the door open with my shoulder. I blundered out, not seeing where I was going. Meatball raced alongside me, barking wildly. He bounced around for a few seconds, sniffing the ground, before he took off.

"Wait! It's not safe." I waved the piece of wood around. It didn't make contact with anything.

Meatball was still barking as he raced away.

I looked up and let out a choked laugh. "You're kidding me. Our assassin was a badger!"

Meatball was in hot pursuit of the giant black-and-white striped creature as it lumbered away into the woods.

I turned and looked back at the door, relief coursing through me. There was no government agent about to get me.

Once my heart returned to a normal rhythm, I headed back to the van, keeping a lookout all the time, just in case any more badgers charged us, or secret agents slid out of the shadows intent on doing me harm.

Meatball appeared in front of me on the path, wagging his tail.

"I hope you chased off the evil brute. I've never been so scared."

"Woof, woof."

I scooped him up and walked speedily to the van. Even though the immediate danger was averted, my nerves were jangling, and I was convinced someone was about to jump out and attack us.

It was only when I was inside the van with Meatball, the door was locked, and we were heading back to Audley Castle that I finally breathed a huge sigh of relief.

"We need to tell Campbell about this," I said. "He has to know that Simone is back in the area. I got so caught up in what she told me that I didn't check her alibi. What if she's involved in these killings and it's got nothing to do with that government site?"

Meatball dropped his chin on one paw as if considering the question.

"Has she been on the run because she killed Eleanor and was worried she'd go to prison for it?"

"Woof, woof?"

"Yes, I'm not sure either. She was frightened. Simone believes someone's after her."

I arrived back at the castle and parked the van. I sat in the seat and wrote a text to Campbell.

Simone Matthews is back. Eleanor's suicide was faked. She was given illegal drugs from the testing site and lost control. It's a big cover-up. You were right.

I sent the message and waited. There was no reply.

Just when I needed Campbell, he wasn't around.

I hurried to Saracen's apartment and knocked on the door.

He opened it, dressed in a robe and fluffy dinosaur claw slippers. "Oh! Holly! I was just about to take a bath."

"Sorry to disturb you. I'm looking for Campbell. Have you seen him?"

"I know where he is. He had to go to London with the Duke and Duchess. He won't be back until the morning. Are you okay? You look worried."

"I need to talk to him. I've found Simone Matthews."

"You did? Where's she been hiding?"

"She's been on the move for years, never staying in one place for long. She told me what happened at the testing facility all those years ago. I sort of understand why she made a run for it."

Saracen rubbed the back of his neck. "I can put in an emergency call to Campbell. We have a way to get in touch with him if it's urgent. But I know the Duke and Duchess were in closed door meetings and then heading to a formal dinner. He may not pick up the message straight away. How quickly do you need to speak to him?"

"Soon. If you can get in touch with him, that would be great. I'm in over my head on this. I can't believe he was right. These murders are linked to the government site."

"Campbell does get things right sometimes." Saracen looked down at his robe and tightened the belt. "Is there anything I can do to help?"

"Let Lee at Marchwood Manor know there could be someone coming after Jacob and Dexter. Security needs to be on the alert."

"You think they'll be targeted tonight?"

"No! I mean, they could. I don't know. They could also be after Emily and Simone, and they're in hiding." I ran a hand through my hair, not sure what to do next. There were too many people who needed protecting.

He touched my arm. "I'll sort it. Lee's an idiot, but he won't ignore intel I give him about the Marchwood family being at risk. They'll be safe overnight. Is there anything else I can do?"

That was a relief. There were times when it was handy having the castle security on my side. "No, you've done enough. Thanks, Saracen. Enjoy your bath. Nice slippers, by the way."

He waggled the dinosaur claws. "A gift from my niece. She's six and crazy about dinosaurs. They're really comfortable."

We said our goodbyes, and I headed to my apartment. I checked my cell phone several times, but got no reply from Campbell.

Gran flung open the door before I had a chance to get the key in the lock. "I was so worried when you didn't send me a message. I almost called the police and sent them out looking for you."

"Sorry! I took a picture of Simone but got caught up in what was going on. Plus, I had to make a hasty exit. It slipped my mind. Everything's okay. And I did find out some useful information."

She gave me a huge hug before leading me into the lounge. "You figured it all out?"

"Almost. Simone and her friends made a huge mistake years ago, and it looks like their secret has been uncovered. I'm handing this over to Campbell. The sooner he's back from London, the better. He can deal with things from now on."

"So long as you're safe." Gran stroked my hair off my face. "You've had enough danger for one day."

I checked my phone again. "I wish Campbell would get in touch. I want to make sure he knows what's happening. Saracen said he'd try to reach him, but—"

"But nothing. You leave the dangerous work to the men with the muscles and guns. You've done enough. You figured out this mystery, now let Campbell tidy it up."

"Saracen is warning Jacob and his friend to stay safe." I chewed on my bottom lip. "The security at Marchwood Manor will look out for them."

"Then you've done everything you can. You can hardly go over to Marchwood Manor and stand guard outside."

I sank back in my seat. "That's true."

She patted my knee. "You need a break. Let me run you a bath. I'll make you some hot chocolate and you can relax. All this nasty murder business is over."

"Thanks, Gran. After the night I've had, I could do with that."

It was almost over. Now I knew why the gang was being killed off, Campbell could use his contacts to find out who'd been killing them and put a stop to it.

I didn't think I'd sleep, but after a hot bath and a warm milky cocoa from Gran, I'd slept for a solid eight hours.

I woke feeling better. This mystery was over. I didn't know if the shadowy government killer would face retribution for what they'd done, or whether it would lead to another cover-up, but that wasn't something I had any power over.

I arrived in the kitchen to find Chef Heston standing by the large to-do list on the board. "Holly, we've had another last-minute order from Marchwood Manor. Sir Richard is hosting an afternoon tea party, and he wants food taken over."

"Oh! I guess I could do that." Marchwood Manor had lost its shine after everything that had happened.

Chef Heston arched an eyebrow. "Don't sound too keen to do your job."

"Of course. Sure, I'll make the delivery. Let me know when it's ready to go."

I settled into my usual routine of baking, happy that my thoughts weren't fixated on murder for a change.

I kept an eye on my cell phone but still heard nothing from Campbell. We'd have to have a talk about his communication skills.

Three hours passed before Chef Heston showed up at my work station. "The order for Marchwood Manor is ready."

"I'm on it, Chef." I grabbed my things and loaded up the van.

I was about to head out but hurried back in the kitchen and grabbed one of my chocolate mocha cream cakes. I'd drop by and see Clive Carrell while I was there. It must have been so hard for him, losing his daughter in such tragic circumstances. Not to know the truth about what really happened to her seemed unfair. But it wasn't my secret to share. Not just yet. The truth would come out once Campbell got everything sorted.

I shot him a quick text. *Did you get lost in London? What's going on?*

I made the short journey to Marchwood Manor. I pulled up and opened the side of the van.

"Holly, I'm glad to see you here." Sir Richard strolled out. "Have you heard that I'm hosting a tea party for some eligible bachelorettes?"

"I didn't know this was a matchmaking party." I pulled out several trays of food and loaded them onto a trolley.

"It was my son's idea. He said I'm rattling around in this place on my own. He has a point. I think that's why I have so many parties. It would be nice to have a lady by my side."

"I hope you find someone wonderful," I said. "Where do you want me to set up the food?"

"Take it through to the kitchen. I'll get the kitchen staff to deal with it in a bit." He walked along beside me as I pushed the trolley. "I'm glad to have something fun to look forward to. After this dreadful business with Adam and Bruce, it put a dampener on things, but my security man is on top of things."

"I'm sure it'll be sorted soon." Well, as soon as Campbell stopped being AWOL.

I headed into the kitchen with him. Sir Richard offered me a coffee, which I declined.

He made himself one and nodded as he surveyed the food. "It looks excellent, as usual. I'll leave you to it. You can see yourself out."

"Thanks, Sir Richard. Oh, while I'm here, do you know if Clive is free? I thought I'd drop in and say hello."

"He should be about. He takes his lunch break roundabout now. You'll find him at the staff apartments around the left side of the house. He's in the third one on the right."

I returned to the van and grabbed the chocolate mocha cake. I walked around the side of the house and discovered the apartments.

The third apartment along had a green front door with a planter full of lavender outside. I knocked and waited. Clive didn't answer.

I walked around the back of the apartments to find neat gardens fenced off. They each had a small shed and a patch of lawn. There was no sign of Clive.

I'd just turned away when there was a thud from inside the shed.

I hurried to the locked door. "Clive? It's Holly. Are you in there? I brought you over a cake."

There were several more thuds and what sounded like a muffled groan.

"Clive? Are you okay?" I balanced the cake in one hand and tried the lock. It was padlocked from the outside. I'd need a key to get in.

I returned to the window and pressed my face close to the glass. The black curtain covering it moved an inch. A pair of wide, terrified-looking eyes stared back at me.

My heart skipped a beat. "Jacob! What are you doing in there?"

He whacked his head against the glass. There was a smear of blood on his forehead. There was a moan and a thump as he disappeared from view.

I needed the key to the lock so I could get him out. I raced to the front of the apartment and peered through the window. I looked in on a small, neat lounge. There wasn't much furniture in there, other than a large recliner chair, a side table, and a TV cabinet. There was a movie playing on the screen.

I stared at it, and my breath whooshed out. That wasn't a movie. That was the video Simone had shown me on her cell phone, playing on repeat.

I took a step back and stumbled over a garden ornament. I almost lost my balance and dropped the cake as I caught myself. I scrambled up and was reaching for the box when the door opened.

Clive stared down at me. "Holly! What are you doing down there?"

"Oh! Nothing. I, um, I brought you a cake." I thrust the slightly squashed box at him. He must know Jacob was locked in his shed. Had he locked him in there?

"A cake? Thanks. Why would you do that?" He stared at the box.

"I ... I was visiting Marchwood Manor and had one going spare. I hope you like chocolate mocha." I glanced at the window. The video was still playing.

A horrible realization settled over me. Clive knew exactly what had happened to his daughter. He knew the conspiracy gang had been there when she died.

Clive glanced at the window. He tensed for a second before scraping a hand over his unshaven chin. "Why don't you come in?"

"Thanks, but I have to get back to work. Chef Heston is expecting me. We're busy this afternoon. I'll be missed."

"Everyone gets a lunch break. I insist. Come inside." His tone hardened and his eyes narrowed.

I thought about running or calling for help, but there was no one about.

Clive reached forward and took my arm. "It'll be nice to have company. I don't get many visitors. People stay away. I think they're worried I'll talk about Eleanor. No one likes to deal with another person's grief."

I nodded slowly. There was no getting out of this. And if I kept him distracted, I could keep Jacob safe while I found a way to call the police, or Campbell, or anyone to help. "Sure. I can spare five minutes."

He took the cake from my hand and ushered me through the door before closing it behind him. "Straight ahead. The kitchen's at the back."

I hurried in front of him, looking around to see if I could grab a weapon or find a way out. I couldn't see anything. I'd have to talk my way out of this one.

"It's a nice place you have here," I said.

"I like it. Sir Richard's been good to me over the years. I know he could easily employ someone younger and fitter, but he keeps me on."

"He must value your work."

"I hope it's the reason I'm still here." Clive placed the cake on the counter. "I hear you've been getting involved in investigating what happened to Adam and Bruce."

"Not really. I mean, a bit. I'm sometimes good at spotting things other people miss. Campbell calls it an annoyance when I try to help."

"I'd say it was unfortunate." Clive let out a sigh. "I take it you looked in the lounge window and saw the video?"

My gaze dipped, and I nodded. "I did."

"And did you also poke around my shed?"

I lifted my head and met his gaze. "Clive, what have you done to Jacob?"

"Given him a taste of what pure terror feels like."

I swallowed, my chest feeling tight. "How long have you known what happened to your daughter?"

His expression tightened. "I'm actually more interested in what you know. Somebody's been telling secrets. Is that why you started looking into me?" He leaned against the counter and folded his arms over his chest. "Who's been talking to you?"

I wasn't telling him anything about Simone. He'd only go after her. "I do understand. Eleanor's death was a tragedy. It—"

"It was a disgrace. She didn't need to die. She was murdered by that group. They were supposed to be her friends. She lost her life because some jumped up teenager decided to teach her a lesson."

"You know everything that happened?"

"I do now. I've always had my suspicions. I could never believe Eleanor took drugs. Sure, kids go off the rails when they're younger. We all like to experiment, drink a bit too much and party too hard. Eleanor was always open with me. She'd tell me if she'd had a drink or if she liked a boy. I felt like the luckiest dad alive because she was honest with me. If she'd ever tried drugs, I'd have known. My little girl must have been so scared when that evil jerk messed with her."

"How did you get the recording?" I said.

"It arrived two weeks before Jacob's reunion party. Bruce sent it to me. He said I needed to see it and it would explain everything. He told me he was sorry. Like that was going to change anything. His sorry did nothing to bring Eleanor back."

"Bruce suffered a lot. Maybe his own health problems had to do with keeping that secret."

"I'm glad. It was no less than he deserved. He's as guilty as the rest of them." Clive looked out the window. "I wasn't sure what I was looking at the first time I ran the recording, but then I spotted Eleanor. I must have watched that thing a hundred times that first night. That's when I realized Eleanor didn't kill herself. They murdered her."

"Is that when you decided to start killing them? You wanted revenge for what happened to your daughter."

"Anyone would have done the same. She was an innocent. Adam always thought he was better than everyone else. Even when he was a teenager, I didn't think much of him. Because he was born with a silver spoon in his mouth, he thought he could take whatever he wanted. And he did just that when he took my daughter's life."

"If it's any comfort, he didn't mean to kill her. Things got out of hand. He took the drugs from that testing site, and—"

"I know. I know it all. I saw the recording, and I heard an audio clip Bruce sent me. I'd kill every single one of them if I could."

"You'd never get away with it."

"I'd give it my best shot. And I've got plans for that government agency and their dodgy drugs. I'm releasing the audio of that night to the public. It'll ruin them."

"Clive, that's dangerous. What if they retaliate?"

"What have I got left to lose? Besides, times have changed. Government agents can't sneak around killing people, even though that's what the idiot security guard here thinks is going on. I was happy to fuel that fire." The rage simmering in his eyes made me cold. "I'd have gotten away with it, if it wasn't for you."

An icy ball of terror lodged in my gut. "You'd never have been able to kill them all."

"I've already managed two. Jacob is next. He's too trusting for his own good. It was so easy to grab him this morning."

"No! Clive, you have to stop. Your daughter wouldn't want this."

"You know nothing about Eleanor. She was an angel. She was my happiness. Ever since her death, I've struggled to find a purpose, going through the motions of living, but never happy. Then the recording arrived, and everything changed."

"Revenge isn't a reason to live. And people know what you're doing."

"No one other than you knows." His hands flexed. "That can be changed."

I backed away around the kitchen counter. "You don't have to hurt me. I never did anything to Eleanor."

"You interfered. You tried to ruin things for me."

"Clive! You did that yourself. I agree that you have every right to be angry. But they were teenagers. Dumb, reckless kids who didn't think through the consequences."

"They had help."

"From the government site. I know. They were wrong to cover this up. They were protecting their work. That was selfish."

"Adam destroyed Eleanor, and his friends helped him. I will have revenge."

I screamed as he lunged at me. I grabbed the cake and hurled it at him. Chocolate mocha cream splattered everywhere as it slammed into his face.

Clive wiped squashed cake off his face. "Holly, I can make this easy on you. I'll make your death quick. I like you. Don't make this difficult."

"I don't want any kind of death." I circled the table, making sure to keep out of Clive's grasping hands. He had murder in his eyes, and it was directed at me.

He threw himself at me and grabbed my arm.

We tumbled to the floor in a mess of thrusting limbs and sticky cake. I kicked, punched, and screamed. Please let someone hear me.

Clive roared. His forehead bounced off mine, then he slumped down, motionless on top of me.

I held my breath. What just happened?

"Holly? Is that you under there?"

"Gran!" I shoved Clive off me. "What are you doing here?"

"I had a bad feeling, so I followed it. I heard you'd come to Marchwood Manor, so decided to find you." She held her right hand out. In her left, she held a large rolling pin.

I grabbed her hand and held on tight. "You saved me."

"Of course. I'll always save you. Holly, why were you fighting this man?" She dropped the rolling pin and hugged me.

I clung to her like a lifeline. "Clive, he killed Adam and Bruce. We must hurry. He's hurt Jacob. He's locked in the shed."

"In the ... shed?" Gran glanced at the back door.

I pulled back, my knees wobbly. "Yes! We have to find the key. And we'll need an ambulance."

"Wait! Sit and take a breath. I'll deal with this." She forced me into a chair, grabbed the phone off the counter, and started making calls. "Hello, we need an ambulance and the police at Marchwood Manor. A man is unconscious and we have a ... a kidnap victim in need of medical help."

I struggled to get my cell phone out of my pocket. I rang Campbell.

"Holmes, where are you?"

"At Clive's apartment at Marchwood Manor. Campbell, he's the killer."

There was a tiny pause. "I'm ten minutes out. Are you hurt?"

I flicked cake off my arm and pressed a fresh bruise. "Not really."

"Stay put. Are you alone?"

"No, my gran's with me. She knocked out Clive."

"She ... okay, not important. Good work, Holmes."

I stared at the mess in front of me. It was work, but I wasn't sure it was all that good. And it wasn't over just yet.

Chapter 21

"Jacob, are you okay?" I caught him as he fell out the shed door, his hands tied behind his back and his legs bound. He had a gag over his mouth, which I quickly removed.

"Holly!" He gasped out my name. "How did you know I was here?"

"It's a long story. Let's get you untied. There's an ambulance on the way."

"I couldn't believe it. Clive said he could do with a hand moving a heavy crate from his shed. Of course, I was happy to help. When I got inside, he whacked me on the head. I passed out. When I came to, I was tied up."

"I've got a lot to tell you," I said. "Come inside."

Jacob hesitated. "Where's Clive?"

"Don't worry about him. My gran's got everything under control."

"Your gran? I don't understand." His gaze went over my shoulder. "Oh! Who are you? The police?"

I turned, tensing at the sight of a man in a black suit standing by the gate. "Can we help you with something?"

His gaze shifted from me to Jacob. "I believe you can. You've been looking into something that doesn't concern you."

"Holly, do you know this guy?" Jacob said. "He doesn't look like a paramedic."

I caught the scent of peppermint and whiskey faintly mingled together. "We've met before. If you're here to threaten me again, you're too late. Your secret's out. People know what happened the night Eleanor died."

Jacob stiffened beside me. "You know about that?"

I sighed. "Jacob, I found out what really happened to Eleanor. So did Clive. That's why he killed Adam and Bruce. He was coming after all of you. He knew about the cover-up."

"There was no cover-up," the man by the gate said. "This is a simple misunderstanding."

"Then why have you been threatening me?" I said. "You warned me off, as did your colleague. If there's no secret to conceal, you wouldn't have done that."

"Why don't you come with me and we can talk?" the man said. "I'll clear everything up."

"More likely, you'll make me disappear just like you want this secret to."

"Holly's not going anywhere," Jacob said. "I don't know who you are, but—"

"You may not remember me, Jacob Marchwood, but I remember you. I was there that night. I know about your friends breaking into the lab and stealing government property. You gave that property to the young lady who died that night. That's not acceptable. You all broke the law."

I gulped. Gran may have gotten rid of one threat, but we had a new one looming in front of us. "The police are on their way."

He shrugged. "The local police force won't be able to help you."

"Maybe they won't, but I know a man who can." I lifted onto my tiptoes as I spotted Campbell charging along the path. "Campbell! Get over here. Don't let this guy get away."

The man took a step back. He glanced over his shoulder just as Campbell charged into him, knocking him off his feet. There was a brief struggle before Campbell had him pinned to the ground.

"Who did you just order me to attack?" Campbell asked.

"He didn't introduce himself, but he's behind the attempts at keeping me quiet and away from this investigation." I kept a tight hold on Jacob as he wobbled on his feet.

"He was threatening us. He was threatening Holly." Jacob cast a guilty look my way. "We're all really sorry about Eleanor. It got out of hand so quickly. I ... I never meant for that to happen. I liked Eleanor. We all did."

"I know. I understand. I've spoken to Simone."

"Simone's here? I haven't seen her since Eleanor died. How's she doing?"

"She's been better. Come inside, Jacob. I need to have a look at your head injury. Campbell, have you got a handle on things out here?"

Campbell pressed down on the guy's windpipe. "This guy's not going anywhere. But we need to talk. It sounds like I've missed a lot."

"Let's deal with the injured first, then we can tidy this up." I led Jacob into the apartment, my mind spinning.

This was never about a big government cover-up, hidden aliens, or conspiracy theories. It was about one grief-stricken man lost in his despair, finally getting the revenge he felt he deserved.

❦❦❦❦❦❦ ❦❦❦❦❦❦

Three hours later, I was settled on a vast squashy red couch in Sir Richard's front parlor. A tray of my chocolate mocha cake was laid out, along with tea and coffee for everyone.

MOCHA CREAM AND MURDER

Campbell was there, alongside an angry looking Lee. Jacob, Dexter, and Sir Richard were also present, and my gran, who was my new favorite heroine.

Alice and Rupert hurried through the parlor door.

Alice flung her arms around me. "We heard what happened. You should have brought me with you. I know martial arts. I could have stopped Clive hurting you."

"I had my amazing Gran as backup," I said. "I was always going to be safe."

Gran sat next to me on the couch, her hands clasped firmly around one of mine. "I taught Holly everything she knows."

Sir Richard stood and paced in front of the fireplace. "I still can't believe Clive killed Adam and Bruce. He must have been out of his mind."

Jacob shifted in his seat. "I can't say I blame him, Dad. What we did all those years ago, it was unforgivable."

"There's never a reason for murder." Sir Richard turned and regarded his son with a stern expression. "You all did wrong by Eleanor. Everyone was led to believe the poor girl's death was a suicide. And all this time you've been hiding the truth."

"It wasn't my proudest moment, Dad. But we were scared. We thought we'd get in trouble."

"You should have gotten in trouble," Sir Richard said. "You ruined Clive's life."

"We never meant for anyone to get hurt." Dexter drained his second large whiskey. "I feel terrible about this. Adam was always in charge of the group, and we felt we had to go along with it. None of us wanted to mess up our futures."

"That's no excuse," Sir Richard said. "You'll have to speak to the police. There'll be questions to answer."

Jacob slumped in his seat. "Of course."

There was a quiet knock at the parlor door. Lee walked over and opened it.

I stood from the couch. "Simone! You're here."

"Is it okay if I come in?" Her gaze skittered around the group. "I heard Clive had been arrested for the murders."

"Of course. Simone, it's been way too long." Jacob strode over and hugged her.

She tensed for a second before returning his hug. "I thought we were all in danger. I thought the government was going to keep us quiet after what happened to ... well, you know."

I looked at Campbell. "Can you give us an update about that? Who's the mysterious guy who's been threatening me?"

Campbell nodded. "His name is Max Redmayne. He used to run the testing facility in Appledore. He works as a consultant these days for the military, setting up labs around the world to run viral testing facilities. He was there the night Adam stole the drugs and gave them to Eleanor. He was the guy who decided to keep things quiet. He's always had an eye out for word that the secret was about to be revealed. He figured he'd stop by and caution people from revealing his dirty little secret."

"He recognized me from that night," Jacob said.

"This Max sounds like a fool. He didn't realize what would happen when he went up against Holly Holmes," Alice said.

"I got lucky," I said. "If Campbell hadn't been there to take him down ..."

Campbell shrugged. "I'm just doing my job."

"Even if Max had silenced me, more people knew about it," I said. "Clive was planning to reveal the truth to the media."

"Clive's also been receiving threatening messages. Scare attempts to make him hesitant before pulling the trigger,"

Campbell said.

"That wouldn't have succeeded. He was never going to give up. Clive was planning to bring down anyone involved in his daughter's murder," I said.

"Including us," Simone said softly.

"That's right," I said. "He had nothing left to live for."

Jacob grimaced as he led Simone to a chair and they sat next to each other. "I really wished it had never happened. I feel terrible about Clive. I still have nightmares about what happened to Eleanor."

"Me too," Simone said.

"What will happen to Max?" I said to Campbell.

"I've spoken to his superiors. They're opening an investigation. According to my contacts, they had no idea Max was trying to keep his name out of the dirt. He won't come after any of you again. I've made sure they're aware we have evidence of the cover-up. If any harm happens to any of you in the future, all that evidence will be leaked."

"Campbell, you're so clever," Alice said. "Thank you for looking after us all."

He nodded, a faint blush rising up his cheeks. "You're welcome, Princess."

"And this all started because Bruce sent Clive the recording?" Sir Richard said.

"It did," I said.

"Things started going wrong for Bruce ever since Eleanor died," Jacob said. "He was a sensitive guy, but that pushed him over the edge."

"I'm sure it didn't help his mental health," I said. "Clive always had suspicions that Eleanor's death wasn't suicide. Although he had no proof, he was certain something bad happened to her."

"The video didn't show everything, though," Dexter said.

"It was enough to get Clive asking around," I said.

"It's likely Clive forced the rest of the information out of Bruce. He got everything he needed and then killed him. He may even have made Adam confess before pushing him off the veranda," Campbell said.

"I'd have been next," Jacob said.

Sir Richard stopped pacing. "I'll put in a good word for Clive at his trial. I don't know if it will help, but he was a decent guy. He can't have been in his right mind, not to have done this. The loss of his daughter devastated him, I remember it so clearly. I'm ashamed my son and his friends were involved in this. I'll do everything in my power to ensure he gets a fair hearing and all the support he needs."

Jacob hung his head. "I wish I could go back in time and change it. I'd do it all differently. I'd have told Adam to stop being an idiot, stop being so mean to Eleanor."

"We can't do anything about the past, but we can make the future as comfortable as possible for Clive," Sir Richard said.

Everyone was silent for a moment as they digested the news.

"We should get you home, Holly." Gran patted my hand.

"Have some of your cake. It always makes me feel better." Alice thrust a large piece of chocolate mocha cake at me.

I gently pushed the plate away. "Thanks. I'm not sure I can eat right now. I wouldn't mind a lie down, though."

"Then it's settled." Alice stood. "We'll take our leave of you. Campbell can tidy everything up. The killer's been caught, and everyone knows the truth about Eleanor."

"Of course, Princess," Sir Richard said. "And thank you Holly, for everything you've done."

"I'm just glad I stopped any more murders," I said.

"I'm glad you prevented mine." Jacob walked over as I headed to the door with Alice, Rupert, and Gran. "Sorry for getting you involved. This is all my mess. I should have sorted it out a long time ago."

I touched his elbow. "Don't be too hard on yourself. Peer pressure is a powerful thing. We do a lot to keep our friends safe. Why don't you start by looking after the ones you still have?" I nodded at Simone, who was dabbing tears off her cheeks with the back of her sleeve.

He glanced at his dad and then Simone. "I've got a lot of making up to do."

I looked around the room. The expressions were a mixture of shock, sadness, and surprise.

"It's time for you to go home," Alice whispered in my ear. "You put yourself in too much danger this time."

"And I'll be right there with you," Gran said. "Let's go, Holly."

I was too exhausted to protest. I nodded at Campbell before being led out of the room.

Maybe it was time to give up on this sleuthing business.

❧❧❧❧❧ ❦❦❦❦❦

It had been three days since Clive was uncovered as the killer. Life finally felt back to normal in Audley St. Mary.

I was whipping up a fresh batch of chocolate mocha cake when Campbell appeared by the back door in the kitchen. "Have you got five minutes, Holmes?"

I set down my bowl. "Sure. What's up?"

"There's someone I'd like you to meet."

I stepped outside, coming to a halt when I spotted a man dressed in a black suit. He had a nondescript face that would easily blend into a crowd. "Is this one of your government contacts?"

"This is Dominic Kelly," Campbell said.

The man nodded. "How do you do, Miss Holmes. I've been liaising with Campbell over the recent incident involving my colleague, Max."

"You know the guy who's been threatening me?" I said.

His lips pursed. "As far as we're concerned, Max had no orders to keep this secret. He wasn't authorized to threaten anyone. That's not how we operate."

Campbell took a step toward Dominic.

He licked his lips. "What I meant to say was I'm here to offer you an apology. No hard feelings for what happened. It's rare, but we occasionally get agents go rogue. They work in high-stress situations and can sometimes lose focus."

"He lost focus enough to assault me and terrify me," I said.

"I apologize for that." Dominic shifted from foot to foot. "When the unfortunate incident with Eleanor Carrell occurred—"

"You mean, when she was murdered because she took a drug you were testing at a facility no one knew about?"

Campbell stifled a smile.

"Let's just say, the incident was a one-off and will never happen again."

"What about the blonde woman who warned me off? Did she work with Max?"

"I'm not certain who you're talking about," Dominic said.

"Quit jerking us around," Campbell said.

Dominic rubbed his chin. "It was most likely his assistant. She was new at the site when the trouble happened. I believe she still works for Max."

"Is she also being spoken to about this … misunderstanding?" I asked.

"Yes, it's all being dealt with. It did highlight certain flaws in our security. But that's beside the point. Max was starting out in his career ten years ago. That was his first big assignment. He was keen to make a name for himself. He knew if word went up the chain of command that he'd let teenagers break into his facility, steal expensive and highly classified material, it would ruin his career. So, he made an error of judgment."

"He covered things up and thought that would be the end of it," I said. "People died because of that cover-up. A man's life was devastated because he thought his daughter killed herself."

"Again, most regrettable," Dominic said. "Because of that, I'd like to offer you something in the way of compensation. Something that'll ensure your silence."

"My silence?" I glanced at Campbell. "I have no plans to tell anyone else about this. Although maybe I should. It seems wrong to have these facilities near people. They aren't safe."

"It would be unfortunate if you did. And very difficult to prove. The word of one kitchen assistant over a government agency." He spread his hands, a smug smile on his face. "It would be looked at as ridiculous."

"Holly wouldn't be on her own." Campbell crossed his arms over his chest. "Dominic, don't be a jerk. Remember what we talked about."

Dominic raised a hand. "Very well. Campbell assured me you're a woman of integrity and always want to ensure justice is done. You've done just that by finding Adam and Bruce's killer."

"There wouldn't have been a killer if your security was better," I said.

"This was a learning experience for us. Max, in particular, is learning from it."

"You haven't … done something to him? I mean, he wasn't a nice guy, but I don't want him dead."

"Oh! No, we don't kill trained agents. That's a waste of resources. Max won't ever be a problem again, that's all you need to worry about."

That wasn't the tiniest bit comforting.

"So, how about this compensation?" Dominic said. "It's for the problems you've had and the stress caused by your unfortunate entanglement in this matter. How does twenty thousand sound?"

"No! I don't want your money. I don't need it." It felt wrong taking their money.

"Holly, you should think about it. The government pays out a lot to keep people quiet." Campbell shot a glare at Dominic. "Much more than twenty thousand."

"That's not our official line," Dominic said. "Officially, we don't give pay outs for this kind of situation, but Campbell can be persuasive."

"I'm not interested in hush money," I said.

"Holly! Don't be stubborn," Campbell said. "You could do a lot with that kind of cash."

"If I take the money, it'll feel like a bribe."

"It's not that. It's simply a way to show we have an understanding," Dominic said.

"Which is also called a bribe." I turned and glared at Campbell. "I definitely don't want any money. However … if you'd like to make a donation to the local donkey sanctuary, I'm sure they'd appreciate it."

"The donkey sanctuary?" Dominic glanced at Campbell. "Is she serious?"

"It's often hard to tell with Holly," Campbell said.

"That's a most unusual request," Dominic said.

I shrugged. "That's all I'm interested in. I'd never spend any money you gave me. It would feel wrong. If you have money to donate to a good cause, then that's what I choose. Can I trust you to do that?"

"I'd have to run this by my superiors. The agency isn't supposed to make charitable donations. This is public money, after all."

Campbell stepped forward and growled. "You'll make an exception, since this is such an unusual case. One-off, didn't you say?"

Dominic tugged at his collar. "Yes, you're right. I'll get onto that right away. And once again, this was a terrible tragedy. You should never have been involved. You won't be hearing from me or my colleagues again. We consider the matter finished."

"Then so do I." I nodded at Campbell. "The donkeys will thank you very much for your generosity."

"Let me see you off the premises." Campbell caught hold of Dominic's elbow and marched him away. He returned a moment later. "Donkey sanctuary? Really?"

"I don't want any dodgy government money burning a hole in my pocket. Besides, it was the first thing that came to mind. Maybe I should have suggested the dog pound, instead?"

Campbell chuckled. "You really are one-of-a-kind, Holmes. You're reckless, impulsive, and have a terrible habit of racing off on your own without backup. And—"

"Hey, that's not fair. I didn't go to Clive's because I thought he was the killer. I was going to offer him comfort. I was just lucky, or unlucky, depending on how you look at it, that I found Jacob in his shed and the video playing on the TV."

Campbell sighed and shook his head. "If you'd let me finish before blurting out the first thing that comes into your head. You were also more level-headed than me in this case. I got embroiled in the conspiracy theory idea. I got distracted by my competition with Lee. I missed the other clues and believed the lines Lee was feeding me."

A smile spread across my face. "You're saying I cracked this case wide open all on my own?"

"You may have given it a hard tap."

"I always knew there was no such thing as conspiracy theories." I turned and headed back to the kitchen, Campbell walking along beside me.

"There definitely are. Most of them are more than theories. It's best you don't go poking around in that nest of vipers. Once you get bitten, there's no cure."

"I've had quite enough of dealing with mysterious government agents. Give me a simple everyday murder any time."

"There's never anything simple when it comes to murder." We stopped at the kitchen door. "Good job, Holmes. Clive has been charged, the police are figuring out what to do with Jacob and his buddies, and you stopped a government agent who'd gone rogue."

"With a little help from my friends."

He smirked, but it was more of a smile. "Now, get me a piece of that chocolate mocha cake."

I laughed as I walked back into the kitchen. There would always be cake, there would always be crime, and there would always be Campbell grousing at me.

Life in Audley St. Mary was never dull.

About Author

K.E. O'Connor (Karen) is a cozy mystery author living in the beautiful British countryside. She loves all things mystery, animals, and cake (these often feature in her books.)

When she's not writing about mysteries, murder, and treats, she volunteers at a local animal sanctuary, reads a ton of books, binge watches mystery series on TV, and dreams about living somewhere warmer.

To stay in touch with the fun, clean mysteries, where the killer always gets their just desserts:

Newsletter: www.subscribepage.com/cozymysteries
Website: www.keoconnor.com/writing
Facebook: www.facebook.com/keoconnorauthor

Also By

Enjoy the complete Holly Holmes cozy culinary mysteries in paperback or e-book.

Read on for a peek at book seven in the series - Lemon Drizzle and Murder!

Chapter 1

"Let's see if the restorers need feeding." I balanced a full tray of leftover cakes and sandwiches in my hands, excitement running through me at the thought of spending an evening immersed in a rare historical discovery.

Meatball, my adorable corgi cross, bounced around my feet, keen to see what delicious food might be available for him.

"There's none for you. You're having dinner soon. Come on, let's take a look in the east turret and see how they're getting on."

Audley Castle was hosting a small team of expert restorers, who were working on a stunning renovation of a ceiling painting uncovered in the old gallery.

I'd put myself in charge of keeping them fed. But really, it was so I could watch their progress and marvel at their finds.

I'd only made it a dozen steps from the back door of the castle kitchen, when Campbell Milligan stepped into my path.

"Holly, what are you up to?" He arched an eyebrow.

"Jeez, give a girl a break. Why are you lurking in the shadows back here?"

"I never lurk. What are you doing with that cake?" He snagged a piece of lemon drizzle cake from the tray.

"Giving it to more deserving people than you. Hands off. I'm going to see how the restoration work is going."

Campbell shook his head as he walked along beside me. "That's a terrible idea. It's a death trap in the old gallery."

"What are you talking about?"

He grabbed the tray out of my hands. "Allow me. That looks heavy."

I narrowed my eyes at him. "So long as you don't eat any more."

"I may have one or two slices of cake. Call it my payment."

"So, the old gallery is a death trap?"

"I've been in there a few times since they started work. It's chaos. There are tools and equipment everywhere. They don't know what they're doing."

"The Duke and Duchess wouldn't allow just anyone into the castle. Herbert Fitzwilliam-Smithe is an expert in art restoration. He's been doing it for thirty-five years. He lectures at Oxford and Cambridge and goes all over the world showcasing his efforts to preserve fragile art."

Campbell snorted. "I forgot you were a history geek."

"There's nothing geeky about history. I can't wait to see how they've been getting on." The restoration crew had been in the east turret for eight days, painstakingly cleaning the ceiling art.

"There are dozens of paintings in the main castle. There's nothing exciting about this one," Campbell said.

"It's been hidden under layers of dirt for hundreds of years. The last time I went to take a look, they'd uncovered a piece of sky. And there were angels. It'll be stunning when it's finished."

He grunted. "Well, just be careful when you're staring at the ceiling. The stairs were wet when I checked on the security arrangements. They're using some cleaning technique that means everything gets soaked. I'm not sure about the guy who's in charge."

"Herbert's sweet. And he knows what he's talking about."

"Sweet's one word for him. The last time I spoke to him, he had his jacket on inside out and his shirt misbuttoned."

"He's eccentric. He's more interested in his work than looking smart. There's no harm in that."

Campbell reached for another piece of lemon drizzle cake.

I smacked the back of his hand. "That's not for you. Give me the tray if you can't control yourself." We reached the entrance to the east turret.

Meatball bounded in ahead, barking with excitement, the sound echoing off the stone walls.

Usually, neither of us were keen to go into the east turret, given its unusual cold spots and strange ghostly whispers, but this time was different.

"Don't say I didn't warn you." Campbell grabbed a piece of cake and strode away before I had a chance to tell him off.

I shook my head, then walked inside. There was a spiral staircase in the middle of the turret that led to Lady Philippa Audley's private rooms, and three large open plan rooms on the lower level.

The old gallery was what interested me the most. A leak on one wall six months ago had exposed a piece of the hidden art. It had been examined, and the family decided to have the whole room updated and restored to welcome even more visitors to the castle.

I dodged around puddles on the floor and several tools and headed into the room.

There was a huge row of scaffolding set along one wall that reached up to the ceiling. There was a woman working up the top in one corner. I recognized her as Sara Silverman, one of the assistant restorers.

"Holly! You're an angel. You come bearing gifts again." Herbert Fitzwilliam-Smithe wandered over, pushing his small, round glasses up his long nose. He definitely fitted the mold of an eccentric historian, with his white hair pulled back in a ponytail and mismatching clothes. But I'd enjoyed the chats we'd had. He knew everything about this particular historical period and was passionate about restoration work.

"I don't want to see you go hungry. And of course, I'd love to have a peek at what you're doing. How's it going?" I nudged aside more tools with the tray and set it down on the painting table.

"We've had an excellent day. We've been using the water washing technique to remove the crusted-on dirt. It means we get a better look at what we're working with. Watch out for the puddles, though. We had a problem with the hose. Justin lost control and sent water everywhere. I'm grateful the walls are made of stone, so they'll dry out. Come take a look."

"Herbert, where's the report I asked you for?" A petite brunette with a cut-glass British accent marched over. She glared at me. "Oh, you're here again."

"Hi, Bluebell. I wanted to see how you've been getting on. Would you like some cake? I've brought lemon drizzle," I said as sweetly as I could. Every time I met Bluebell Brewster, she looked at me as if I was something unpleasant she'd found on the sole of her shoe.

She peered down her nose at me. "Herbert, the report? I have to submit it to Greta. We're already two days late getting the information she needs."

Herbert smoothed a hand over his unruly hair and his cheeks flushed bright red. "Of course. I got side-tracked by an incredible discovery. Apparently, the layout—"

"I'm not interested in layouts. Focus on your task. You have to provide the reports to show we're making progress. We can't waste our funder's time, or they'll withdraw their support."

"They won't stop funding us." Herbert smiled and nodded. "This is too important."

"They will if we don't tell them what we're doing," Bluebell said.

His warm smile faded. "Of course. I'll get right onto the report."

"You haven't even started it?" Bluebell scowled at him. She was at least ten years younger than Herbert but was definitely the boss around here. "Greta will be here soon. She won't be happy to hear about this."

"Oh! Don't tell Greta. She doesn't understand our work." Herbert flapped a hand in the air.

"She understands finances, which is why she's overseeing this project. If you keep messing up, she'll get rid of you. I don't care how many PhDs you have, or how many years lecturing to wide-eyed students. We work in the private sector now. That's where the money is."

"I think Herbert and his assistants are doing a great job," I said. "If you brought your funder to see the progress, they'd be interested. They wouldn't want to stop this from being finished. It'll be so beautiful when it's done."

Bluebell glanced at me. "What's your specialty again?"

"Holly studied history at university," Herbert said. "She's got an interest in our work."

"And yet she works in the castle kitchens," Bluebell said. "Isn't it time you got back to your baking and stopped distracting my work crew?"

Meatball raced over and bounded around Bluebell, leaping up and pressing his damp paws onto her pristine pale gray pants.

"Ugh! What's he doing here?" Bluebell stepped back into a pool of water and scowled. "For goodness sake. Herbert, clean this place up and get on with the report. If I have to ask you again, I'll rethink the management structure and send you back to the university." She turned and stalked away.

"Oh dear," Herbert said with a sigh. "Bluebell doesn't seem happy with me. She's a demanding woman."

From the adoring look in his eyes, that wasn't all he thought about Bluebell.

"Is that cake?" Justin Banderas bounded over on long, thin legs. He gave me a huge smile as he shoved his scruffy, shoulder-length brown hair out of his eyes. "I'm starving. Thanks, Holly." He set to work on a huge slice of lemon drizzle cake, his free hand reaching for a sandwich.

"You're welcome. It would have only gone to waste. We can't keep things like this overnight because it doesn't stay fresh." I grinned as Justin continued to shovel in food. He definitely needed filling out. He was rake thin. And from the threadbare appearance of his clothes, I got the impression he didn't earn much. I doubted assistant restorers ever got rich. They did this work because they were passionate about it.

"Sara, come down. Holly's brought us food," Justin yelled, covering his mouth to avoid splattering everyone with crumbs.

Sara turned and waved a hand in acknowledgement. She unclipped the safety harness that attached her to the scaffolding, then climbed down a ladder. She walked over, wiping her hands on a cloth before tucking it into the waistband of her pants.

"Great. I've been working up on that scaffold all day. I'm famished." Sara Silverman was the opposite of Justin. She was short and plump, with round cheeks that were speckled with freckles and shoulder-length red hair.

"How's the restoration work going?" I said.

"Come take a look," Sara said. "I'm proud of what we've uncovered."

I followed her to the bottom of the scaffold with Herbert and Justin.

"Justin, switch on the spotlight. The light's fading." Sara grinned at me. "Or you can shin up the ladder and take a look if you're feeling adventurous."

"Don't go up there." Justin wheeled over a large spotlight and aimed it at the ceiling. "It's horribly high. You'll never get me up to the top."

"It's not so bad when you get used to it," Sara said. "You're missing out on all the fun."

He shuddered. "I have no head for heights."

Sara squeezed his arm. "Don't worry. I'll do all the high work. Take a look at that, Holly. We think this could be an original painting from Witkor Alderman."

"I've heard of that name," I said.

"He was famous a few hundred years ago. He was everyone's go-to guy when it came to creating elaborate works of art in hard to reach places. He was like the Banksy of medieval times. There are numerous cracks in the original plaster work, but this will clean up well," Sara said.

Justin munched on a sandwich as he adjusted the spotlight and beamed it on the painting. There were dull splashes of blue and white, along with what may have been an arm.

"Holly! There you are."

I turned just as Princess Alice Audley shrieked, skidded in a puddle of water, and landed flat on her back.

Herbert gasped, and Justin dropped his sandwich.

I raced over with Sara to help Alice up.

"Are you okay?" I grabbed her arm.

"Oh! Princess Alice, I'm so sorry." Herbert rushed over. "I should have signs up. Bluebell's been telling me to put up the hazard markings, but I've been distracted by some fascinating research about Audley Castle."

Alice accepted his hand and pulled herself upright before brushing down the back of her soaked pink dress. "Don't worry about me. I never look where I'm going. I'm almost as bad as my dopey brother. Holly, I was hoping we could have dinner together tonight."

"Oh, sure. I'm free. I was just having a look at the restoration work."

"Campbell told me you were here." She glanced around. "He also told me to be careful. Don't mention my little trip to him. He'll only tell me that he told me so."

"Our secret's safe," I said.

"Princess Alice, I'm so glad you're here," Herbert said. "I've been reading about the legendary gold chalice that inspired the painting on the ceiling. I believe that when the work is finished, we'll find a depiction of the chalice. Wouldn't that be remarkable?"

"You're talking about the Audley goblet?" she asked.

"That's it. Some people call it a goblet, some call it a chalice."

"Or a bowl," Justin said as he took more cake. "No one's sure what it actually looks like."

Herbert nodded. "There are all sorts of fascinating theories about its origins, and where it's been hidden."

"I've never heard about this chalice," I said.

"It's a myth," Alice said.

"There's often truth in myths," Herbert said.

"Tell that to the Loch Ness monster." I grinned at him.

"She was a real beast," Herbert said. "Although monster hunting isn't my specialty, I have a colleague at Exeter University who has visual proof of the creature."

"I'd love to see that," Alice said. "Holly, we should arrange a visit. And we can take Herbert's friend with us so he can point out the best viewing spots."

Herbert chuckled. "Ah, I don't think you'll find Nessie alive any longer. She'd be hundreds of years old. But I can have him send you some photos."

"Oh, that's not such fun," Alice said.

"What about the Audley chalice?" I said. "You said that no one's ever seen it."

"Not for hundreds of years," Herbert said. "It's believed to be made of solid gold and embedded with rubies and sapphires."

Justin whistled. "That would be worth a lot of money."

"A fortune," Herbert said. "There'd be a huge amount of interest in the historical community if it was ever found."

"It's not real," Alice said. "Granny sometimes mentions the goblet. She's convinced it's hidden somewhere in the castle. I've looked everywhere. I'd know if there was a priceless chalice hiding anywhere."

"Imagine what you could do with all the money if you sold it," I said.

"Build another castle," Alice said. "One with fewer drafts and walls that don't leak."

"I'd have a new wing of the university built and named after me," Herbert said. "The Herbert Fitzwilliam-Smithe lecture hall. That has a ring to it."

"I'd pay off my student debts," Justin said. "And move out of my dingy apartment."

"Same here," Sara said. "Then go on a luxury cruise."

"You could do a lot more with the money than that," Alice said. "But as I keep saying, it's not real."

"I hope we do find a depiction of it once we've removed the dirt on the painting," Herbert said.

Alice wandered about, flipping up the waterproof sheeting covering the statues around the old gallery.

She uncovered one and patted its head. "My great-grandfather will be looking on with interest. But you'll be disappointed if you're hoping to find the goblet."

"A painting of it would be enough for me," Herbert said. "It would prove its existence."

"Or it would prove someone had an active imagination a few hundred years ago," Alice said. "Come on, Holly. I'm starving. Let's go have dinner. I've ordered a delicious treat from the kitchen."

I shook my head. "Chef Heston won't be pleased to know he's providing my dinner tonight."

"He'll get over it. He always does. His bark is worse than his bite."

We said goodbye to Herbert, Sara, and Justin, and headed out of the old gallery.

Meatball raced after us, bouncing around me.

"I know. It's dinner time," I said.

"I haven't left Meatball out," Alice said. "I ordered him a special bowl of braised beef and vegetables."

I groaned. "Chef Heston will kill me. Now, he's feeding Meatball, too."

"He loves cooking. And I didn't say the food was for you and Meatball."

"He'll know. He always does." I dodged around Meatball as he continued to bounce in front of me. My foot hit a piece of pipe sticking out from under a cloth.

I grabbed my toe and yelped.

"What's the matter?" Alice said.

"My toe! I just whacked it." I hopped on one foot, wriggling my sore toe. My foot slipped from under me on the wet stone.

Meatball dodged around me, and I pitched over, smacking my head on the damp wall.

Everything went fuzzy for a few seconds, then an icy touch drifted across my cheek.

I twisted my head, but there was no one beside me.

I rolled over, blinked several times, and came face-to-face with a skull.

Lemon Drizzle and Murder is available to buy in paperback or e-book format.

ISBN: 978-1-9163573-6-5

Here's one more treat. Enjoy this delicious recipe for a binge-worthy mocha coffee traybake. Granny Molly approved!

Recipe – Mocha Coffee Tray Bake

Prep time: 15 minutes **Cook time**: 25 minutes

Recipe can be made dairy and egg-free. Substitute milk for a plant/nut alternative, use dairy-free spread, and mix 3 tbsp flaxseed with 1 tbsp water to create one flax 'egg' as a binding agent (this recipe requires 9 tbsp flaxseed to substitute 3 eggs.)

INGREDIENTS
3/4 cups (175g) butter
3/4 cups (175g) caster sugar
3 eggs beaten
1 1/2 cups (175g) plain flour
1 1/2 teaspoon baking powder
2 heaped teaspoon coffee granules
1 tablespoon boiling water
Mocha Drizzle
1 1/4 cups (150g) icing sugar
1 tablespoon cocoa powder
1 heaped teaspoon coffee granules
1 teaspoon butter

2 tablespoons boiling water
Walnuts to decorate

INSTRUCTIONS

1. Preheat the oven to 190C/170 fan/375F.

2. Grease a 10x8 inch tin and line with baking paper.

3. Cream together the butter and sugar until light and fluffy.

4. Add the beaten eggs a little at a time, mixing well.

5. Fold the dry ingredients into the wet mixture gently. Don't over stir.

6. Place mixture into the tin.

7. Bake for 20-25 minutes, or until the top is golden brown and springs back when pressed, or a toothpick comes out clean.

8. Let cool (try not to eat it all in one sitting!.)

9. When the cake has cooled, mix the drizzle ingredients until thick. Use a teaspoon to drip over the cake.

10. Stud the frosting with walnut halves and serve.

Printed in Great Britain
by Amazon

27051733R00138